P9-CPY-433

Darby grabbed on to the saddle horn. The gelding's ragged breath was all around her when she fell forward on his neck. She didn't release her grip on the horn, even when it jabbed her ribs.

She stayed on long enough that Navigator stopped bucking, but he was running again, this time at a reeling, unsteady gait.

As the gelding homed in on a section of fence, she thought he was going to try to jump out of the round pen.

Then, Darby saw that she was wrong.

Good, steady Navigator was about to rub her off on the fence.

Check out the
Phantom Stallion
series, also by Terri Farley!

1

THE WILD ONE

2

MUSTANG MOON

3

DARK SUNSHINE

4

THE RENEGADE

5

FREE AGAIN

6

THE CHALLENGER

7

DESERT DANCER

8

GOLDEN GHOST

9

GIFT HORSE

10

RED FEATHER FILLY

11

UNTAMED

12

RAIN DANCE

13

HEARTBREAK BRONCO

14

MOONRISE

15

KIDNAPPED COLT

16

THE WILDEST HEART

17

MOUNTAIN MARE

18

FIREFLY

19

SECRET STAR

20

BLUE WINGS

21

DAWN RUNNER

22

WILD HONEY

23

GYPSY GOLD

24

RUN AWAY HOME

Welcome to

Phantom Stallion

WILD HORSE ISLAND

1

THE HORSE CHARMER

2

THE SHINING STALLION

3

RAIN FOREST ROSE

4

CASTAWAY COLT

5

FIRE MAIDEN

6

SEA SHADOW

Phantom Stallion

WILD HORSE ISLAND 5

FIRE MAIDEN

TERRI FARLEY

HarperTrophy®

An Imprint of HarperCollins*Publishers*

Disclaimer

Wild Horse Island is imaginary. Its history, culture, legends, people, and ecology echo Hawaii's, but my stories and reality are like leaves on the rain forest floor. They may overlap, but their edges never really match.

Harper Trophy® is a registered trademark
of HarperCollins Publishers.

Fire Maiden

Copyright © 2008 by Terri Sprenger-Farley

All rights reserved. Printed in the United States of America. No part of this book may be used or reproduced in any manner whatsoever without written permission except in the case of brief quotations embodied in critical articles and reviews. For information address HarperCollins Children's Books, a division of HarperCollins Publishers, 1350 Avenue of the Americas, New York, NY 10019.

www.harpercollinschildrens.com

Library of Congress catalog card number: 2007936701
ISBN 978-0-06-088618-9
Typography by Jennifer Heuer
❖
First Edition

This book is dedicated to Sharron Faff,
Hawai'i Volcanoes National Park ranger

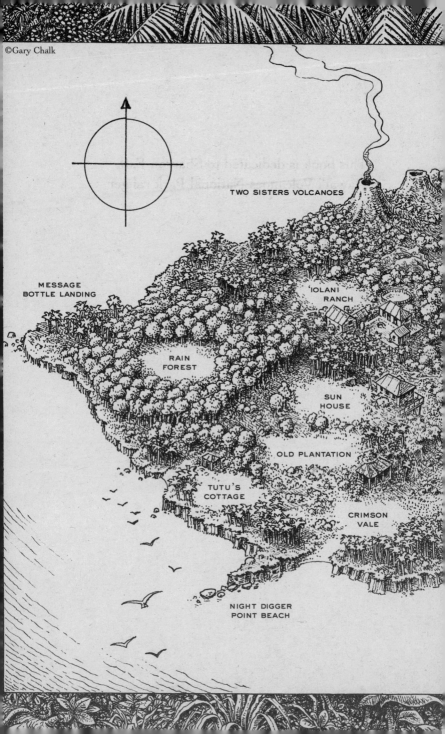

©Gary Chalk

TWO SISTERS VOLCANOES

MESSAGE
BOTTLE LANDING

'IOLANI
RANCH

RAIN
FOREST

SUN
HOUSE

OLD PLANTATION

TUTU'S
COTTAGE

CRIMSON
VALE

NIGHT DIGGER
POINT BEACH

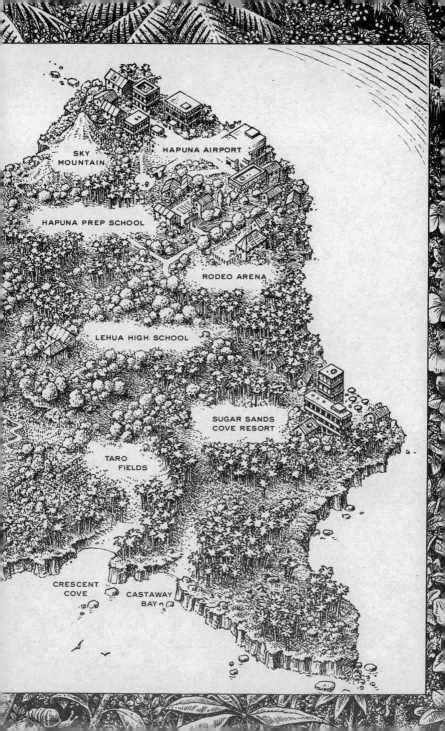

Chapter 1

"My foreman tells me Hoku is about ready to start carrying a rider," Jonah said as Darby Carter climbed out of the 'Iolani Ranch truck after school.

Although her boots had just now touched the red Hawaiian dirt, and she still held the truck door open, Darby didn't move. If she'd slipped through time molecules into an alternate reality, one in which her grandfather trusted her to start riding her mustang filly, she didn't want to change position and shatter this dream come true.

Darby took in everything around her. It looked just like it had when she'd left for school that morning.

She was still in Hawaii, on Wild Horse Island.

The Australian shepherds were barking their usual welcome, and Sun House—in which she had a bedroom—was still cantilevered over a bluff, looking down on hundreds of emerald acres that made 'Iolani Ranch heaven for horses.

Across the yard, in one direction, sat the round pen.

Past it, right where it should be, stood the foreman's green house next to the tack shed. Beyond that, a clutter of grayed wooden fox cages rested in the shade of a tree that often provided a hunting perch for a friendly owl. And right on down the path, she could see the corral where her filly Hoku was penned, getting used to the sights, sounds, and smells of ranch life until she was . . .

"Kit said Hoku's ready to carry a rider?" Darby finally repeated.

"It's not April Fools' Day, Granddaughter," Jonah told her. "He said she did fine in the waves over at Sugar Sands and he doesn't think we should waste her curiosity."

"Wow," Darby said.

Jonah looked like he was holding in a smile.

As Megan Kato, Darby's best friend on the ranch, slid down from the truck carrying her soccer bag, she gave Darby a thumbs-up.

"Go change your clothes and meet Kit at Hoku's corral," Jonah said.

Megan flashed Darby an excited look and said, "This is so cool. I'm coming over there to watch."

"Hurry," Jonah urged, as if Darby had settled in for a chat instead of shivering with anticipation. Then he glanced at the horizon and added, "This might use up all the daylight we've got left."

Use up all the daylight? Darby caught her breath.

Was Jonah forgetting that she and Hoku had an unpredictable relationship? Most of the time, they were sisters. Once in a while, though, the mustang filly regarded Darby with the same impatience she had for other clumsy two-legged humans.

With raised eyebrows, Darby looked at Aunty Cathy. Although Cathy Kato was Megan's mom and the ranch manager, and not really related to Darby, the woman was a respected friend that Darby honored in the Hawaiian way by calling her aunty. Besides, Cathy was an experienced horsewoman and Darby always welcomed her advice.

Pushing her brown-blond hair out of her eyes with the back of her wrist and balancing a bag of groceries on her hip, Aunty Cathy said, "I wouldn't count on teaching an untrained horse to carry a rider before dinnertime, but that's just me."

"Hmph," Jonah said. "Probably right. That filly's got too much wild horse in her. She'll just run off instead of standing and thinking like her dam."

Hoku's dam was Princess Kitty, a running

Quarter Horse related to the champion Three Bars. Jonah believed Quarter Horses were royalty in the world of equines.

Jonah gave an approving nod for his own wisdom, then walked away before Darby could speak up for Hoku's mustang bloodlines.

In a mock-Western accent, Megan drawled, "Ya got 'til sundown, Horse Charmer."

"I really want to do this, but a little warning would have been nice," Darby muttered as she looked after her grandfather.

"Tell him you want to wait," Cathy suggested. "At least until after your camping trip."

Darby's sensible side, the part of her that had ruled her life when she lived in Pacific Pinnacles, California, agreed with Aunty Cathy. She'd only been riding for a month, after all.

But Darby's Hawaiian heart, the part of her that had come to life on Wild Horse Island, overruled her head.

"No way!" Darby said, and she ran inside Sun House, down the hall to her bedroom, to pull on riding clothes.

Ten minutes later, Darby was jogging toward Kit Ely. The ranch foreman, a half-Shoshone Nevadan who was often mistaken for a Hawaiian, stood at the fence of Hoku's corral. In his customary chaps and pressed shirt, Kit looked younger than usual as he gave Darby his happy wolf smile.

This is going to be fun, Darby thought, and just then, her horse moved out from behind Kit.

Ears pricked at the sound of Darby's approach, the sorrel filly tossed her flaxen forelock from her eyes. Her hooves made a staccato beat as background to her snorts and nickers.

She's glad to see me, but she wants Kit to go away. Because the filly had been beaten by a man during her colthood, Hoku had good reason to dislike men, but she tolerated Kit better than other males.

"Hi!" Darby heard her own singing tone as she walked up to the pair.

Kit's smile showed white against his dark features. He looked almost as excited as she felt.

"This is just the beginnin'," he cautioned Darby. "Just preparation for the main event, okay?"

"Okay," Darby said, smooching at Hoku.

The sorrel stopped. She flung her muzzle toward her back, as if urging Darby to come inside the pen.

"Listen up now," Kit said, more seriously than before.

Darby let the smile fade from her lips. Crossing her arms to keep in her exhilaration, Darby faced him.

"All we're going to do today is show her how it's done. Riding, that is," Kit said. "Together, we're going to lead her into the round pen and turn her loose, wearing just her halter. Next, you'll go inside, leading Navigator, and I'll bring you your gear and you'll tack him up."

"What will she do?"

"With luck, she'll be watching, feeling just a little jealous."

"Okay," Darby said, and she felt her smile creeping back again.

"Then you'll walk away from Navigator, leaving him ground-tied, and come talk to me. At that point, we hope she'll mosey over to sniff out the dress-up outfit her human has put on another horse. Then you'll get on him and ride around."

Darby's crazy heartbeat began to slow down.

It was enough of a challenge that it probably would take all afternoon and early evening. But the way Jonah had greeted her, well, she'd thought that someone had swung a magic wand over Hoku's golden back, making her instantly rideable. Of course, such a thing could never happen. The wild filly trusted Darby. For now, that was the best she could hope for.

"It's a small step," Kit admitted, "but tomorrow we'll move on. We're buildin' on everything you two been puttin' into each other since you met. Got it?"

"Got it!" Darby said, and she was thinking each step would go faster than Kit thought it would, because no one but her knew of the day in the rainforest corral when Hoku had practically asked Darby to climb on and ride.

She hadn't done it that day because she would have been alone if something had gone wrong.

Now, she had Jonah's approval and Kit's supervision. She wasn't going to waste a minute.

Darby grabbed the tangerine-and-white-striped lead rope that Kit had placed over the fence. Hoku's halter was clipped onto it and the headstall was unbuckled.

As she slid back the gate's bolt to enter Hoku's corral, she noticed that Kit was holding a coiled rope. Hoku noticed, too.

Prancing with high-held knees, the filly peered over the fence and gave a doubtful snort.

Darby clucked her tongue. Hoku ran a single lap around her corral, swinging her head from side to side like a wild stallion, then slid to a cow-pony stop in front of Darby.

"Yeah, you really scared me, didn't you?" Darby smiled. The filly's brown eyes glittered with mischief. "You're just playful because I've been at school instead of giving you my undivided attention, huh, baby?"

Holding the halter open with both hands, she approached Hoku. The filly glanced at Kit, but then took a step forward to meet Darby, and lowered her head. A little.

Darby had to stand on tiptoe to fasten the halter buckle, but Hoku's quick breaths told her the filly was eager to do something.

"Both hands on the rope," Kit said. "One up near her chin and the other about halfway down."

"I know," Darby said.

"I know you do, but she's pretty keyed up. If she decides to take off, she's gotta know you're going to act like an anchor."

Darby nodded, and Kit waited until she and Hoku had cleared the gate before coming toward her with his rope.

A wind carrying the scents of cinnamon-red dirt, lush grass, and stream-wet rocks blew toward them and Hoku breathed man-smell in with the others.

Hoku flattened her ears for a full minute, but Kit came no closer until the filly noticed—at the same time Darby did—that Kit was singing. Darby couldn't make out the words, but the foreman sung in a minor key.

The melody was oddly familiar and reminded Darby of a flute song meant to hypnotize cobras.

Hoku wasn't hypnotized, but as soon as her ears pricked up with curiosity, Kit moved in to snap on his rope. The filly allowed it, sniffing at the leather fringe on his chinks before pawing impatiently, telling Kit that he'd better move away from her, out to the very end of the rope. Soon.

Kit did exactly that, then matched his steps to Darby's.

The filly walked between them, neighing at Navigator as they passed. The dark gelding with rust-colored hair around his eyes was tied to a ring by the tack shed.

Though it only took the three of them a few minutes to walk uphill to the round pen, Darby felt hot and sweaty. The air was humid, but the breeze had stopped. She lifted her shoulder to wipe off a bead of sweat that had dropped from her brow to her cheek.

Hoku kept looking back at Navigator and calling to him.

"She knows today's different," Darby said quietly.

"Mustangs are smart," Kit agreed.

Darby smiled in agreement. She was so glad Kit felt that way. And he was from Nevada, where most of the world's wild horses lived, so he was an expert.

Not that it changed Jonah's opinion.

Even though her grandfather lectured everyone about the wisdom of saddle horses keeping their wild edge, so that they could think for themselves, he didn't believe mustangs like Hoku were particularly intelligent.

Jonah would stake his life on his belief that Quarter Horses were equine Einsteins.

"I'm gonna run ahead and open the gate. You got her?" Kit asked.

"Sure."

As soon as Kit dropped his end of the rope, Hoku edged toward Darby, and then she eased into a jog, head lifted.

Darby trotted alongside her, keeping up as she teased, "Are you glad he's gone, you bad girl?"

Hoku blew her warm breath toward Darby.

Once Kit had the gate open, he returned to help Darby lead the filly through.

Hoku rolled her eyes as if something about him had frightened her. As soon as Kit picked up his end of the rope, the filly rose in a half rear, jerking up all the slack.

"Oh, no!" Darby had hoped Hoku would stay calm and playful, despite the hot, still weather and the break in her routine.

"Don't worry." Kit dodged the filly's flailing hooves as if she were a kitten. "Once we unsnap these ropes, she's gonna forget this part. She'll see you comin' in, leadin' Navigator, fussin' with Navigator, and she's gonna think that's what upset her. She'll come sniffing around to see why you're leaving her out."

Kit's prediction came pretty close.

Megan and Aunty Cathy were watching, arms crossed atop the fence, as Darby tried to saddle Navigator while Hoku interfered.

When Darby worked on the gelding's left side, Hoku approached from his right. She sniffed his nose and Navigator sniffed hers. Hoku nuzzled the gelding's sleek coffee-colored neck, and his lips brushed her golden mane.

Hoku breathed in the scent of the saddle blanket, but kept moving alongside Navigator. She stayed close enough that he began scratching her back with short, firm bites.

Darby stood holding the heavy Western saddle,

poised to fling it on, when Hoku's teeth closed on the saddle blanket, slid it off the gelding's back, and proceeded to groom the gelding with short, firm bites of her own.

Although she heard Aunty Cathy and Megan laughing, Darby held her amusement in, because she saw Jonah approaching and he didn't look pleased.

"Shhhhhoo!" Darby hissed at Hoku. The snaky sound was one the filly didn't like, and she moved off in time for Darby to put down the saddle, replace the blanket, and swing the saddle onto Navigator's back before Jonah entered the corral.

Hoku squealed a "how dare you" reprimand at Jonah when he slid the bolt closed behind him and stood talking to Kit.

"Go ahead and mount up," Kit called to Darby.

She did, but she was aware of Hoku aiming betrayed snorts her way.

For a long time, probably twenty minutes, Hoku stood with her tail turned toward Darby and Navigator as Darby rode the gelding at a walk, jog, and lope.

Once, as Darby rode past, Kit said, "Good goin', Darby. See ya later, I'm pickin' up some hay in town."

It wasn't long after he left that Darby felt Navigator's gait shift from smooth to choppy.

At first she blamed it on herself, but she was pretty sure she hadn't changed the way she was riding. She glanced at Megan, still standing at the rail, and noticed her friend frowning at the gelding's uneven steps.

When she came abreast of Jonah, Darby stopped the gelding.

"Something's wrong with Navigator," she told her grandfather.

Navigator nuzzled the front of Jonah's shirt, but he pushed the horse away.

"Keep him at a jog."

Darby swung Navigator away from Jonah, and urged the dark brown gelding into a jog around the open-air arena.

She was bouncing more than usual in her saddle, so she tried not to watch as Hoku followed Navigator.

"It's not the horse," Jonah said as Darby rode past.

But it was. Maybe it was the muggy weather, or Hoku dogging his steps, but Darby knew Navigator's stiffness and the way he sawed his mouth against the bit was not her fault.

"I trained that gelding myself. It's either you or that broomtail," Jonah said, pointing.

"No way," Darby said. Trying to believe Jonah was joking, Darby smooched at Hoku as she and Navigator jogged past.

But Navigator wasn't joking. The Quarter Horse

moved from a walk, to a jog, then a lope, at her command, but every gait felt as if his legs were jointless wood.

Jonah studied her riding position.

"He thinks he's bound for the racetrack, the way you're up on his neck like a jockey," Jonah told Darby. "Sit back."

"Okay," Darby said, and for a few seconds, she felt at home in the smooth leather seat. Maybe it had been her fault after all.

"Now, jog."

At once, Darby's teeth slammed together.

It was like Navigator's muscles resisted the movement of his bones.

Darby fought to relax. Maybe her tension was telegraphing down the reins to Navigator.

You're a good horse, she thought to the gelding. *And riding is my favorite thing. Hawaii is my favorite place. I can see green grass growing right up to the arena fence and an old bay horse named Judge is grazing so peacefully, a mynah bird is perching on his withers. Past him, I can see mountain peaks wearing halos of clouds, and . . .*

Navigator extended his stride, then veered toward the center of the ring.

Darby swiped at the sweat on her forehead. Neither she nor Navigator could relax, and the April afternoon felt like it was holding its breath.

"Keep him on the fence," Jonah ordered.

Navigator's ears flicked back as Darby adjusted her reins.

"Good boy," Darby told him.

Hoku neighed and rushed from one side of the round pen to the other.

"Get centered. You're leaning left. Sit back." Jonah's voice was charged with frustration. "Ignore that filly."

She tried. She stared at the space between Navigator's ears instead of turning toward the thump of Hoku's hooves.

The next time she and Navigator swept by Jonah, her grandfather frowned.

"Stop," he said.

Darby's fingers flexed. Navigator halted.

Sunstruck dust motes turned gold all around them, but they only made Darby sneeze.

Jonah's black hair glinted silver at the temples and his stride was certain as he approached.

Navigator danced in place. He swung his head so that Darby could see the froth on his lips.

Jonah held up a hand and the gelding lowered his head.

Jonah walked around the horse. Starting at the hooves, moving up over fetlocks, bone, and sinew, his analytical eyes examined each bulge and dip beneath glossy horse hide. He considered bridle straps and saddle buckles, and finally said, "Try holding a rein in each hand. Look down at your saddle horn."

"Okay."

Darby waited for Jonah to return to his place by the gate.

Her grandfather's back was as straight as if a steel rod lay along his spine. She wasn't sure what he was thinking. That she was the only Kealoha on earth not born to be a rider? That he shouldn't have gone along with Kit's idea to turn Hoku out into the round pen while they rode?

Or was he, just maybe, silently agreeing with her that something was disturbing the dependable Quarter Horse?

"Don't keep him going in circles. Pick a post across the arena and ride to it. Then do it again. Not the same place, though. Mix it up."

Darby tried, but the very first time she sighted a fence post and rode for it, the gelding wrenched his head to the right and came in sideways to the fence.

"Why'd you let him do that?" Jonah said incredulously.

Before Darby could answer, Navigator froze in place, ears pitched so far forward, Darby listened for whatever he heard.

Hoku was doing the same thing, and both horses shivered as if flies crawled over every inch of their skins.

"He's shaking," she told Jonah.

"Cluck him up. Put him into a lope and keep him there."

Navigator bounded forward, pretending he was about to lope, before breaking into a gallop.

Hoku joined him, running alongside so closely, her shoulder bumped Darby's stirrup. They were running too fast, slanting like motorcycles on a track.

Faintly, she heard Jonah's warning tone repeat, "Lope."

Head level, teeth ringing on the bit, Navigator began to buck.

Darby grabbed on to the saddle horn. The gelding's ragged breath was all around her when she fell forward on his neck. She didn't release her grip on the horn, even when it jabbed her ribs.

She stayed on long enough that Navigator stopped bucking, but he was running again, this time at a reeling, unsteady gait.

As the gelding homed in on a section of fence, she thought he was going to try to jump out of the round pen.

Then, Darby saw that she was wrong.

Good, steady Navigator was about to rub her off on the fence.

Chapter 2

"Whoa!" Darby shouted.

At the word, Navigator stopped. It was that stop, so sudden a brick wall might have materialized in front of him, that sent Darby somersaulting over his shoulder into the dust.

The first thing she heard was Hoku's curious nicker, but Darby didn't move to look at her horse.

Head. Neck. Shoulders. Back. Knees. Ankles.

Darby reviewed her shaken body and decided she wasn't hurt.

But she was embarrassed, so when she saw Jonah start toward her, she scrambled up and began brushing at her jeans. She blinked grit from her eyes, trying to understand why Navigator still stood fretting beside her.

Jonah eased a hand under Navigator's saddle and tugged the corners of the saddle blanket before ordering, "Get back on."

A wrinkle in his blanket wouldn't make Navigator act like this, Darby thought, and she opened her mouth to tell Jonah that when he said, "Back on, now."

"Could he be afraid of something?" Darby asked, almost whispering.

"Let him be afraid while you're on his back. He's never pulled that"—Jonah indicated the fence Navigator had charged—"before." Jonah held Navigator's reins while Darby climbed back on. "I don't want this horse to think he can throw people."

"You're some role model," Darby told Navigator. "What if Hoku thinks—"

Darby stopped. She wasn't amusing anyone, not even herself.

Shaking a little, Darby climbed back onto Navigator. As soon as she did, she felt how his mood had changed. Not improved, exactly, she thought as he followed the fence line at a flat-footed walk. Loud exhalations made the gelding sound weary, though he let Darby prod him into a jog and, finally, a lope.

When her grandfather signaled her to stop and dismount, Darby led Navigator behind her. The gelding's head drooped and he hung back at the end of his reins.

"Are we taking a break?" Darby asked.

Jonah rubbed his eyes, then said, "I don't have a safer horse on the place."

Darby stopped. What did Jonah mean?

"Navigator's just having a bad day," Darby suggested.

They couldn't quit now. *It's a small step,* Kit had said, *but tomorrow we'll move on.* So, they couldn't end this small step early, or riding Hoku would be delayed, too.

Jonah kept walking toward the gate, until it seemed he couldn't stand the ringing of her last statement in his ears.

"Navigator's having a bad day?" Jonah mumbled. "Granddaughter, I wash my hands of you."

Hoku stood pressed against the farthest fence until Jonah left the corral. Then she trotted to the gate and lingered there, eager to leave the round pen.

Great, Darby thought, as she led Hoku back to her own corral. Now her filly was afraid of the round pen, where she'd get her first lessons in carrying a rider.

When she returned for Navigator, the gelding— for some reason she couldn't imagine—wanted to remain just outside the round pen.

Trying to stop the endless tape that ran through her brain saying *Granddaughter, I wash my hands of you,* Darby let Navigator have his way. She hand-grazed the gelding for so long, dusk crept in. At last,

Navigator's nerves calmed enough that his teeth clipped the grass around her boots and he gave her knee a nudge.

"I know you're sorry."

Wind moaned through the telephone wires. She heard a far-off moo and a horse scratching its neck on a fence.

A skylark's silhouette swooped across the sky, reminding her that it was getting late. She should hurry back to the tack room, strip off Navigator's gear, and turn him loose for the evening.

Jonah was disappointed in her, but it really wasn't her fault.

She hadn't ridden any worse today than she usually did.

When they reached the tack shed, Darby put a neck rope on Navigator, slipped off his bridle, and asked, "What had you so spooked?"

Navigator backed against his neck rope.

Maybe he wanted to escape her question, Darby thought as she looped the bridle over the horn, and carried the saddle into the tack room. When she returned, Navigator's ears were pricked to attention.

Darby didn't hear anything unusual. More than likely, the gelding had just focused on the click of grazing teeth. All around them, animals were eating. Navigator had already forgotten whatever had scared him in the round pen. Dinner was what really interested him.

The gelding had backed as far as his neck rope would allow when Kimo, one of the 'Iolani Ranch cowboys, drove up on a sputtering ATV. Navigator jumped forward as if it wasn't a sound he heard every day.

"I was about to turn you loose, but I know Jonah would make you settle down first," Darby told the gelding as he rolled his eyes.

Kimo climbed off and stretched the kinks out of his back. "Tomorrow's your last day before school's out for spring break, yeah? And then your trip is all planned."

"Yeah," Darby said.

Yesterday she could have matched Kimo's smile, because she was so excited about the overnight ride and camping trip she was going on with Megan and her new friend Ann. A school assignment had triggered the idea of riding up the slope of Two Sisters, but that wouldn't keep them from having fun.

Apparently Jonah had allowed educational field trips and scientific research on his half of the Two Sisters volcanoes for years. His sister, Babe Borden, hadn't been so generous because she was afraid she and Sugar Sands Cove Resort would be sued if someone was injured.

"Yeah, it's all planned," Darby repeated, but she was worried that Jonah might change his mind now, and she couldn't shake her uneasiness over Navigator.

Maybe Kimo could help her figure out what was bothering the big gelding.

"I'm a little worried about 'Gator. He's not sick or hurt," she put in quickly. "He's just not acting right."

Kimo made a sound of agreement. He didn't look a bit surprised.

"Been happening with all the animals all day," he said.

"Really?"

"This morning, before work, I went fishing. Why, I wonder, are the fish out in the middle, in the sun, instead of under the bank?" He shrugged. "And some with no business jumping? They're leaping like the water's too hot for 'em. Weirder still, the chickens at our house? They're roosting up in the tree. Won't come down to their coop, even to eat."

"What's going on?" Darby asked.

"Change in the weather," Kimo guessed. "Cade was having trouble with cattle, too."

Darby looked around. She didn't see Cade, the fifteen-year-old ranch hand and Jonah's unofficially adopted grandson. And Kit hadn't yet returned from the feed store. Not that that meant anything. Once in a while, the foreman stayed in town for dinner at a Mexican restaurant he liked.

Still, the ranch yard was quiet, but she felt the tense atmosphere, too.

Trying to tease her out of her troubled mood, Kimo said, "Maybe a storm's on the way and your vacation will be all rainy, yeah?" He looked pleased when she rolled her eyes at him.

As Kimo drove off toward the home he shared with his father, Darby took a final look at Navigator, then gave him a pat and turned him out.

The horse almost fell in his eagerness to escape. He ran between two of the dogs, Sass and Jill. The blue merle Australian shepherd just wagged his tail, but Jill gave a cranky yap and glared at Navigator as he bolted down the road, swung right, and disappeared toward the pastures below.

Although she was almost afraid to check on Hoku, worried the horse wouldn't be glad to see her because of the round pen uproar, Darby couldn't stay away.

As she walked to Hoku's corral, the two dogs fell in on each side of her. Jill, usually the least affectionate of the dogs, leaned her head against Darby's knee, making her wobble as they walked.

Even though it had been less than an hour since she'd touched her horse, Darby felt the same wonder she did each time she looked at Hoku. The filly's image always went straight from Darby's eyes to her heart.

Backlit by the sunset, the filly's mane shone yellow gold and her coat was coppery, but she looked as nervous as a zoo animal as she paced, halting at each fence as if she'd never seen it before.

Hoku greeted Darby with a worried whinny. Sass

closed his eyes and sniffed, and the horse snapped her teeth on the fleeting breeze.

What did the animals sense?

Darby stayed quiet, trying to read her filly's body language, but Hoku felt her watching. For the first time in weeks, the mustang was unsettled by Darby's stare.

"Do you blame me for all that stuff?" Darby asked, nodding toward the round pen.

Hoku licked her lips and champed her jaws. She looked young and a bit frightened.

"I don't get it," Darby told her horse. Then she released a heavy sigh. "But I'm not helping, am I?"

Darby took a few experimental steps away from her horse. Hoku lowered her head and blew through her lips, relaxing as Darby moved away.

She didn't have to be a horse charmer to see that Hoku didn't want anyone around.

As she walked away, Darby heard Hoku pacing again. The filly moved as if she had no choice, as if her hooves had to measure off the minutes to something she dreaded.

Although she heard birds chirping good night to the setting sun, and knew she should rush to wash the dirt and horse hair off her hands before helping with dinner, Darby made one more quick detour.

She wanted to talk to her friend Megan.

Darby didn't know when Megan and Aunty Cathy had stopped watching at the round pen fence, but they'd seen part of what had happened. Maybe Megan, who'd grown up with horses, would have some insight into Navigator's meltdown.

Darby was climbing the steps up to Megan's apartment, which had been built atop Sun House, when a step seemed to bow away from her boot. Darby grabbed the handrail for balance and wished her stomach would rejoin the rest of her.

What was that?

Feeling dizzy, Darby looked across the ranch yard. The bird on Judge's withers flew away. The dogs began barking. Then Aunty Cathy burst out of the house yelling.

"Megan! Help me catch the goat!"

Darby jumped back as the apartment door opened. Megan gasped in surprise at Darby's nearness, said hi, and laughed as Darby flattened herself to one side to keep the other girl from running her down.

A trim athlete who smelled of coconut suntan lotion, Megan was a head taller than Darby and usually pretty sensible. Because Aunty Cathy was shouting for Megan to hurry, Darby didn't grill her friend about Navigator, but she couldn't help asking, "Did you feel anything just now?"

"Just the earth moving—"

"Really?"

"—from my mom screaming for me," Megan finished as Aunty Cathy started up again.

"Megan! I need you down here!" Aunty Cathy sounded sharp and impatient. The stairs rocked beneath Darby as Megan pounded down the steps to join her mother.

"Do you want me to help?" Darby called after them.

"Watch dinner," Aunty Cathy said, pointing toward the house, and then she and Megan were running.

Chapter 3

Darby burned the rice, but she didn't feel too bad, because Jonah shook extra soy sauce on the pork he was frying. It tasted almost too salty to eat.

As they cooked, side by side, Darby could tell Jonah wasn't angry with her. He was disappointed, though, and that was worse.

"I wasn't blaming anything on Navigator," she told him. "I really do think something's wrong."

"Don't let this horse charmer idea take too tight a grip on you," Jonah said carefully. "Reading equine minds? That's something only another horse can do. We both know that."

Was she trying to read Navigator's mind? Darby didn't think so, but Jonah had been called a horse charmer long before she had, so he probably knew what she was feeling.

The way he'd talked to her about it had been, for Jonah, downright gentle. Because of that, Darby didn't share Kimo's remark that all the animals were acting weird. She wanted to get Jonah's opinion on why, but she didn't want him thinking that she believed something eerie was going on.

Just then, Aunty Cathy and Megan came back into the kitchen, breathless and red-faced.

"You let that goat go off that way, she's gonna run off all her fat," Jonah observed.

Aunty Cathy and Megan gave him tolerant glowers, probably because they'd had to work so hard to catch Francie. Darby sent her grandfather a look that said she'd caught his reference to Francie's fat, and there was still no way she'd go along with his idea for a goat barbeque on the Fourth of July.

After dinner, Darby couldn't shake the feeling that she'd forgotten something. She walked from the kitchen to the living room, paused by Jonah's library, then stood in the center of her bedroom, hoping something would trigger her memory.

She was about to slip out of the house and see if she'd forgotten something out in the ranch yard when a dog began howling.

Jonah gave a groan. He'd just tugged off his boots and didn't want to put them back on again to go outside.

"I'll go see what's wrong," Darby said.

"Lucky for them," Jonah told her, then added, "Thanks."

Perspiration prickled out on Darby's forehead, and something in the atmosphere—maybe barometric pressure—made her feel as if she was trapped in a mummy case of hot air.

As she closed the door behind her, the howling stopped, but Darby heard something else.

Was someone digging over by the foreman's house? She headed in that direction.

When she reached the house, she realized she'd been picturing Kit or Cade at some ranch task, but the one doing the digging was Cade's Appaloosa, Joker.

The gelding's gray-white coat looked as it always did, as if someone had sprinkled him, nose to tail, with licorice drops.

Mischief wasn't in Joker's mood tonight. Head down, nose almost touching the lowest porch step, the gelding pawed the dirt.

Hatless and barefoot, Cade leaned in the doorway with his arms crossed. Inside light poured past the teenage paniolo, spotlighting his horse.

"What's he doing?" Darby asked.

Cade shook his head. "Can't say."

Joker barely glanced at Darby when she clucked quietly, then walked near enough to touch his shoulder.

"He's sweaty. Has he been running?" Darby pulled her hand away and shot Cade an inquiring look.

"Nope. He's been at this awhile," Cade said.

Darby recalled Kimo's remarks about the odd behavior of fish, chickens, and cattle, and then there'd been Navigator and Hoku. Now, Joker.

She was pretty sure Cade wouldn't scoff, so she said, "Kimo thinks the weather's about to change, and that might be why the animals are acting up."

"He could be right," Cade said. "Kit and I took forever moving a few head of cattle."

Just then, Bart, the youngest of the Australian shepherds, came skittering across the yard. His tongue lolled from his mouth as he bounded up onto the porch.

Darby jumped back as Joker clomped up the lowest stairs. He was trying to reach Cade, too.

Darby heard heavy steps from inside the house.

"What's this, now?" Kit shouted at the racket of hooves and claws.

In a single stride, the foreman was outside, shooing with the book he carried, and both animals backed noisily down the steps. But they didn't leave. They stayed near Darby, instead of running away.

"If you want that Bart as a pet, I can't blame you," Kit told Cade, "but I don't think you'll make a lapdog outta the Appy."

"It's not like I invited them in," Cade protested.

"Don't mean nothin' if you did," Kit told him.

"I'll go lock up the dogs," Darby said. "That's my job, anyway."

Staring westward into the starry sky, Kit nodded slowly. Darby wondered what the foreman would say if she told him his long black hair and turquoise necklace made him look like a Shoshone shaman.

She didn't have the nerve to find out, but she smiled to herself until Kit said, "I expect we'll know what's got 'em all riled up by morning. All I know's I'm sleeping in a chair tonight. And I'm not takin' off my boots."

Darby awoke inside a seashell.

For a few groggy moments, she thought she was dreaming. She lay on her side, cheek pressed against carpet. The room around her was no bigger than a closet. Bookshelves climbed the walls, spiraling toward an arched skylight.

It was the light streaming onto her childish pink nightgown that convinced Darby she was awake. The sleeveless garment was decorated with a white horse. That part was fine, but the horse carried a disproportionately huge prince and princess and the script beneath them, which hadn't completely washed off, read, SLEEPING BEAUTY.

She might someday outgrow the nightgown, but it was still the lightest thing to wear in warm weather.

Darby knew where she was now: in Jonah's library.

Last night, she'd had a hard time falling asleep. Her mind had darted from her fall off Navigator to Jonah's disapproving frown, to howling dogs, to the gnawing thought that she'd forgotten to do something important.

So she'd reread her favorite mystery, hoping she'd fall asleep. Instead, she'd climbed out of bed around midnight and crept into Jonah's library in search of a book to replace the one she'd finished.

What a cool place to fall asleep, Darby mused. Her eyelids closed. On the verge of dozing off again, Darby remembered what she'd forgotten last night.

Oh, no. Darby bounced to her feet, ducked through the library's rabbit hole entrance, and crawled into the living room. She kicked the door closed behind her and darted to the bench by the front door, where she'd left her backpack. With fumbling fingers, she unzipped the backpack and snatched out the handout for her Ecology class partner project.

No. No. No, she moaned silently.

Two sections of the partner project were due today. Ann had agreed to do an experiment that demonstrated something about volcanoes, if Darby would interview Tutu about volcano stories. Ann's part of the assignment required her to photograph three stages of the experiment and post it on the class website no later than midnight. Without looking, Darby was sure Ann had done her part.

But Darby had let Ann down.

Navigator and Jonah and hitting the ground—
No. Darby stopped herself from making excuses.
Navigator's odd behavior and her own disgrace were
no reason to forget her schoolwork. She was a better
student than that.

But what should she do now? Darby stopped
pacing in the living room and forced herself to go
look at the kitchen clock.

It was five thirty. Still early. Very early.

What if she ran outside, saddled Navigator, and
galloped through the rain forest to Tutu's cottage?
She might have time to get there and back, but that
wouldn't leave more than a few minutes to talk to her
great-grandmother about the intertwining of stories
and science as they applied to volcanoes. And if
Darby was late getting back to the ranch, she'd be
late for school. And if she was late for school, Megan
would be, too.

There was no fix for it, Darby decided. She'd
have to throw herself on Mr. Silva's mercy and beg
her teacher to let her turn in that part of the project
along with the third part, their field observation on
Two Sisters, after spring break.

"If I still have a partner," Darby muttered to herself.

Ann was not going to be happy. The red-haired
Nevada girl was a dedicated student, just like she
was. And though Ann would understand that Darby

had been distracted by horses, she would probably be disillusioned by her new friend's slipup.

"So, what's for breakfast?"

Darby whirled away from her contemplation of the clock to see Aunty Cathy. In jeans and a crisp white shirt, with her hair curled because she was going into town for something Darby couldn't remember, Aunty Cathy regarded her with such an understanding smile, Darby began confessing how badly she'd messed up.

"Hmm," Aunty Cathy said as if she were thinking. "Does it have to be your tutu?"

Darby blinked a few times, then reached for the class handout.

"An elder," Darby read, then looked up.

"Sadly, I fit that description," said Aunty Cathy. "And there are some stories my husband Ben and his friend Pani used to try to scare me with; that might be what you're looking for. . . ."

"Thank you!" Darby launched herself at the woman, hugging her neck with both arms.

"You haven't even heard them!"

Darby didn't care. Having help was what mattered. It struck her that Aunty Cathy smelled like gingerbread—a little sweet, a bit spicy, and the next best thing to a mother.

When Darby finally released her, Aunty Cathy kissed Darby's cheek.

"I don't promise it will work," she cautioned,

opening the pantry door, "and since I need a few minutes to think, what if I make us some French toast with peanut butter and jelly, while you hurry through your feeding chores?"

"Okay," Darby said reluctantly.

"We've got time. Just race right back here with your notebook as soon as you're finished with the animals."

Since speed was important, Darby decided no one would notice if she pulled on her jeans and tucked in her nightgown like a blouse. After that, she jammed her feet into sneakers.

"I'll be right back," Darby called to Aunty Cathy.

Outside Sun House, she noticed Joker was already tied by a neck rope to the hitching post. Francie the goat was bouncing on all four hooves at the end of her tie chain and bleating, tattling on Kona, Jonah's big gray Quarter Horse, as he nosed open the feed-room door.

Darby spotted Jonah striding across the dewy grass toward Kona. She cupped her hands around her mouth to shout, but the words were knocked out of her mouth and out of her mind as she slipped, landing on the seat of her jeans.

For a millisecond, Darby was embarrassed.

Then she recognized 'Iolani Ranch's slow-motion sway.

Earthquake, Darby thought. A sound like distant waves blotted out every other noise.

Life halted in a silent freeze-frame.

Joker reared up. Hoku's head, mouth agape, showed above a fence. Megan must have run down the stairs from her apartment at the first shake, because she was poised on tiptoe. Her little dog Pip was clamped under her arm.

Darby's fingernails clawed through the grass beneath her, into the dirt, trying to hold on to the undulating earth as she watched her grandfather.

Jonah's mouth was open for what seemed like minutes before his shout set everything back in motion.

"Cut him loose!" Jonah pointed at Joker.

The Appaloosa's rearing body formed a *C*, contorted by the rope tied to the rack. Cade's knot held against hundreds of pounds of plunging horse.

Dogs yapped without ceasing. As Cade staggered toward his horse, Bart, the youngest Australian shepherd, reached the top of the cyclone fence surrounding the kennel and sprang into the air.

How had he managed to climb so high when the other dogs were trapped?

Bart hit the ground, rolled, then shook himself before cringing for forgiveness at Jonah's feet. Openmouthed and low to the ground, he begged Jonah to make the shaking stop.

Her grandfather didn't notice. He glanced at Darby, then bellowed, "Let her go!" and pointed toward Hoku's corral.

Let her go? Darby's incredulity turned to action when she saw Hoku's golden legs hooked over the top rail.

"Open all the gates or they'll break legs trying to climb out!" Jonah yelled.

He was right. Hoku heaved herself higher and the madness in her eyes was easy to understand. For a wild horse, the open range offered shelter, but she was trapped in a corral. Safety meant the herd, but she was alone.

If Hoku could not escape, she'd die trying.

Chapter 4

The earth still swayed beneath Darby as she ran.

From the corner of her eye, Darby saw Joker fall. He slipped sideways under the hitching rack and his hooves hammered the wooden posts.

Cade crawled toward his horse. A knife slashed through Joker's neck rope. Cade ducked, arms crossed over his head to protect himself from the Appaloosa's flailing hooves.

Kona had vanished, but his muffled neigh and the commotion of heavy things falling meant the feed-shack door had closed behind the gray, trapping him inside.

Should she release him before going to Hoku?

The idea had barely formed when Kit dashed in

front of her. He was braced to open the door when Kona's heavy hooves splintered it from the inside.

As Kona broke through, Kit jumped up and held to the top of the door. He hung on as the door slammed open and the horse rushed by.

Hoku screamed. Spotting Darby, the filly raced to the gate, then rammed it with her chest.

"I'm here! Girl, I'm here!" Darby told her horse, but Hoku crashed into the wooden gate again.

Trying not to think of the splintered feed-room door, trying not to flinch at the acid panic burning through her filly's veins, Darby shoved against the bolt and slid it to the right.

Hoku knocked the gate wide open. Darby dodged the filly's charge just as a black-and-white shape—Francie!—dashed past Megan. The girl dropped Pip and tackled the trailing end of the goat's chain. Pip barked and scampered, an animated mop following her mistress as she was dragged by the frantic goat.

Jonah was yelling at her to let go, but Megan hollered back, "Hang on 'til she—"

The goat looked up to see Hoku bearing down on them.

The wild horse took in the blur of beings blocking her path. Instinct told her she could outrun the chaos. She only faltered for a stride or two before gathering herself to jump.

"Look out!" Darby yelled.

Francie dropped in a faint, then tumbled a few yards, unconscious.

In a moment of silence, Hoku sailed over the goat, girl, and Pip. She landed amid dust that had been kicked up by Joker when he scrambled clear of Cade and the hitching rail.

With her own feet steady beneath her, Darby was pretty sure the earthquake was over, but the horses were taking no chances.

Joker flew like a spotted Pegasus, jumping off the bluff to a trail down below. She hoped his legs could take the impact.

Silently, Darby begged her horse not to follow Joker.

Hoku turned her head almost upside down in an effort to see and comprehend what the gelding had done, but she veered away from the edge and galloped down the road.

Don't go straight to the highway. Oh, please don't.

Hoku didn't. Her slender legs slanted as she swerved to the right. Then, her hooves hammering on the packed dirt trail, she ran down to join the other horses.

Only then did Darby realize her fingers had locked in front of her mouth in a kind of desperate praying.

She ran to the edge of the bluff to look down on a pasture with a single knot of horses.

Fences hadn't kept the broodmares and foals, the

saddle horses, yearlings, and stallion—all the horses on the ranch—from coming together. The multicolored herd broke open to accept Joker, and then Hoku.

All the horses faced inward, turning their tails to disaster.

Nearby, rolling truck tires skidded to a stop. It had been headed for the bluff's edge, too, Darby thought, as she heard the sound of its parking brake being yanked on.

Jonah climbed out of his truck and scanned his surroundings for another calamity.

"It's done," Kit said matter-of-factly. He rubbed his shoulder and added, "Good thing I got one arm workin'."

Darby thought of Kit swinging from the top of the feed-room door as Kona rammed out, and shuddered as she remembered his other arm had been damaged in a rodeo accident. If Kit's grip hadn't held, he would have been trampled.

"Glad I had my knife," Cade said, looking back at the hitching rack as if Joker was still plunging to escape.

"I can't believe he didn't pull up that rack," Darby said, almost to herself.

"Was that worse than we've ever had?" Cade must have been talking to Jonah, but he looked down at Bart.

Ashamed, tail wagging low and eyes wincing at

his misbehavior, the dog pawed at Cade's boots, then rolled over.

Cade cleared his throat and squatted to rumple the dog's black ears.

"That don't look too good," Kit said, considering the lopsided foreman's house.

Something had given way in the little house, but it was the sound of Megan crooning to Pip as she swept the shaggy dog back into her arms that drew both Darby's and Jonah's attention.

"You girls are both okay, yeah?" Jonah asked. He looked them over with a care he hadn't aimed at Cade or Kit.

"I am, but my poor baby was scared." Megan kissed Pip's head.

"Everyday stuff to you, huh, L.A. girl?" Jonah raised his black eyebrows, but his smile looked—not curious, Darby thought—proud.

Darby lifted one shoulder in a shrug.

"I'll go let out the rest of the dogs," Darby said, suddenly aware of the whining Australian shepherds still locked in their kennel.

"There you go," she said, after freeing them.

Jack jumped up to lick Darby's face, but the others streamed toward Jonah.

"You're welcome," Darby said. Gently she slid away from the paws Jack had planted on her shoulders and he joined the other dogs, swirling around Jonah's legs as he stared off the bluff, down at the horses.

"We'll let 'em settle down and gossip about what happened," he said, nodding toward the group of horses, still tightly gathered together. "Kimo will be here soon, if he can be."

Jonah paused for a second, frowning, and Darby remembered that the house Kimo shared with his father was built on the lip of Crimson Vale.

"You don't think the earthquake could've caused a landslide or something, do you?" Darby asked.

"That place's been up there forever," Jonah said, brushing aside her concern, "and so has my mother's, but I'll check on her."

Tutu! Darby pictured her great-grandmother's cottage in the rain forest. She glanced around at 'Iolani Ranch's trees. They all stood firm, but they were probably younger trees. Did that mean the ones surrounding Tutu were more or less likely to be shaken loose from their roots to crash to the forest floor?

"If I can use Tango, I'll get on my way," Jonah said.

"Sure," Megan said.

But as Jonah fought his way into the tack room, shoving the door against a blockade of saddles and grain sacks, Megan looked over the dog in her arms to shoot Darby a glance.

Neither of them could believe Jonah planned to just wade into a herd of nervous horses and catch one that had been running wild for two years.

As if he'd heard their thoughts, Jonah said, "She's fast and she knows the rain forest." He threw a saddle and bridle into the back of an ATV. As he settled them into place, he noticed the dogs sniffing the breeze and did the same. "Anyone smell smoke?"

Frowning, they all sniffed.

"Might," Kit said, then turned to Darby. "You didn't leave anything on the stove, right? It was too early to be cookin'?"

"No . . . ," Darby said, but ugly ideas were clicking into place in her mind.

"My mom," Megan said faintly.

"Where's Cathy?" Jonah demanded, but he didn't wait for an answer.

He ran toward Sun House.

As Megan sprinted after him, Darby felt sick, then desperate to help.

Kit caught her arm and held her back.

"She's fine," he said. "The boss'll shout in a minute to tell us so."

"I've got to go." Darby pictured the crammed-full pantry. And Aunty Cathy.

The earth had come alive and trapped her in there, alone.

Kit stared into Darby's eyes. He released her arm as if he'd glimpsed the reflection of everything in the pantry avalanching down on Aunty Cathy.

"Okay, then," Kit said, but Darby was already running.

❀ ❀ ❀

Broken glass sparkled in a pool of red. It was the first thing Darby saw as she entered the ranch-house kitchen. She stopped, blinking as her mind tried to make sense of what she saw.

Stepping gingerly, Jonah and Megan moved ahead of her.

Behind her, Kit said, "Ketchup."

When the word registered, Darby let herself breathe again.

Kit was right.

Earthquake-rattled cabinets had emptied glass, condiments, and silverware onto the kitchen floor. The refrigerator door stood open. Inside it was practically bare. Mangoes, carrots, and greens of all sorts lay over plastic containers that leaked brown, red, and yellow stuff into a puddle spreading from upside-down ice trays.

"Mom!" Megan shouted.

Darby didn't see Aunty Cathy anywhere.

"Check the pantry," Darby said.

"We heard something moving in there." Megan sounded tearful.

"Stuff could be shifting—" Jonah cautioned, but he was cut off by a clatter and clash.

He sidestepped as a huge can rocketed out of the pantry, spinning across the floor.

"Ow!" Aunty Cathy said as she edged out of the pantry and bent to rub her foot. Judging by the can's velocity, Aunty Cathy had kicked it on purpose.

When she saw the mottled swelling over Aunty Cathy's cheekbone and around her eye, Darby was pretty sure she knew why.

"Watch out," Aunty Cathy cautioned. "That stuff that looks like snow is rice." She stepped over the jumbled canned goods and shards of pottery on the floor. "Before it hit me, that can took out my green rice crock."

"Are you hurt?" Jonah asked, but Aunty Cathy couldn't answer. Megan grabbed her mother in a hug and Darby joined her.

"Mom, I was so worried," Megan said.

Jonah cleared his throat and Darby glanced up and noticed that he looked like he wanted to be part of their group hug.

Instead, he said, "You girls, don't break any bones the quake missed, yeah?"

"I'm bruised, but nothing's broken." The finger Aunty Cathy aimed at the big can was trembling, but her voice was merely exasperated. "Can you tell me why we're storing a can as big as my head—and I got a good, close look at it!—full of pumpkin?"

"No idea." Jonah's black mustache quirked up at one corner.

Aunty Cathy sniffed back tears and Darby knew she'd been using grumpiness to cover her relief.

"Ma'am, you'll have a black eye, 'less you get ice on that," Kit warned. He snatched a bag of frozen peas from the heap of food around them, and held it out.

"It's not even bleeding. Look. It's a white shirt," she said, holding it away from her body. "It would show. I don't think —"

"Ma'am," Kit said again, "pardon me, but I saw a bull rider get hooked by a head-tossin' Brahma and he didn't bleed, either. Still, his face swole up like a red balloon."

"Mom," Megan said. Then, tsking her tongue as if she were the parent, Megan took the cold bag and applied it to the side of her mother's face.

"Thanks," Aunty Cathy sighed.

She closed her eyes, and Jonah snapped, "See a doctor. Today."

Darby thought of everything that had happened on 'Iolani Ranch—pulled muscles, burns, sprains, cuts, and abrasions—but no doctor or vet had been called. She'd never seen Jonah so troubled.

"Competition for medical care," Darby blurted. When everyone looked at her for an explanation, she added, "There might be some."

She remembered the phrase from an earthquake-readiness brochure she'd read in Pacific Pinnacles. The section had been illustrated by sketches of broken buildings, and cartoon figures on crutches with their heads swathed in bandages.

Aunty Cathy's eyes widened. "I almost forgot. Darby, we've still got time to talk about . . ." Her voice trailed off. "What was it, now? You needed it for your . . ." Aunty Cathy's hand spun in midair as she searched for the right word.

Megan leaned toward her mother as if she might need help.

Aunty Cathy kissed her daughter's cheek, then explained, "Don't worry. I'm just going to be Tutu's story stand-in for Darby's Ecology class. She has a homework project due on volcanoes."

Megan nodded, encouraging her mother to continue these logical sentences, until a thought struck her and she interrupted, "If we even have school today."

Kit lifted the kitchen radio, dangling off the counter by its still-plugged-in cord, then clicked it on and tuned it to its usual station.

Within minutes, they'd learned that the earthquake had registered 6.0 on the Richter scale with an epicenter in an undersea volcano that was called by a number rather than a name.

"Early reports indicate minor injuries and property damage on the Big Island and Moku Lio Hihiu . . . ," the announcer said, but soon he was reading off school schedules.

Lehua High School was apparently undamaged, so school wasn't canceled, but it was delayed by two hours, with a ten o'clock start time beginning with Nutrition Break, and no lunch break.

"Of course they couldn't give us an extra day for

spring break," Megan complained, but then she took in the mess surrounding them and sighed. "I can help you get started on this, Mom."

"Me too," Darby offered.

"No," Jonah said. "You go down to the lower pastures with Cade. He can check the cattle while you bring up Hoku—"

"What about Tango?" Megan asked.

"With luck, the others will follow Darby. If not, I'll work something out."

No pressure, Darby thought, but she didn't roll her eyes or complain.

Thumbs in his back pocket, the foreman listened patiently, waiting for Jonah to issue his instructions.

"Check the foundations, the weight-bearing walls, pipes, anything that might come crashing down on us, or shift out from under us."

"Got it, boss," Kit said. He touched the brim of his black felt hat and turned to leave.

"Kimo should be along to help," Aunty Cathy put in, as if the job Kit had been given was too much for one.

"Gotta do something with this adrenaline rush," Kit told her.

Then, as he passed Darby, Kit winked.

As if it's no big deal that Jonah put the safety of every person on this ranch into his hands, Darby thought, looking after the foreman. *As if he didn't mind that he couldn't go check on the girlfriend Megan said he had in town.*

Just then, scratching and whining came from overhead.

"Pip," Aunty Cathy and Megan said together.

"I don't even remember putting her down!" Megan gasped.

Aunty Cathy lowered the bag of frozen peas from her cheek and said, "I'll just run up there and—"

"Let Megan do it," Jonah said. "You can, yeah?"

"Sure." Megan lifted her chin, ignored her mother's wordless protest, and left.

"Bring me some horses," Jonah told Darby.

"Sure." Darby responded as confidently as Megan had, until she realized she still wore her pink nightgown in place of a shirt. "I'll just go change. And I should call my mom and let her know I'm okay."

"Do what you like, but don't give your filly a chance to reach the highway." Jonah considered the disordered kitchen, then said, "Who knows what it's like in town."

"Okay," Darby replied.

Looking ridiculous was nothing compared with putting her horse in danger.

She grabbed a hair elastic she'd left on the entrance hall table, and was gathering a ponytail, when Jonah's low voice reached her.

"Cathy, how does it look?"

"The can bounced off my cheekbone. It's swollen and red."

"Your forehead?"

"Is fine."

Why would Jonah needle Aunty Cathy like that, asking her to describe what he could see with his own eyes?

When his voice turned even quieter, Darby held her breath to listen.

"Just rule out a concussion. Do me that favor, can't you?"

"Yes, Jonah," Aunty Cathy said.

As Darby ran from Sun House to grab Hoku's lead rope, she decided Aunty Cathy must be in shock. Despite her protests that she felt just fine, there'd been something soft in Aunty Cathy's voice that Darby had never heard before.

At the bawl of a siren in the distance, Darby forgot everything but her horse.

 Chapter 5

Darby still felt a little shaky as she walked down the path to the lower pastures. She was determined to catch Hoku and a saddle horse for Jonah, but she wished she'd called her mother before she'd left the house.

Oh well, she'd do it when she got back.

When she heard footsteps, she glanced back and saw Cade following her.

One glance told her the young paniolo was up to something. Cade was the most unpredictable person she'd ever met. Reading horses' minds was a million times easier than figuring him out.

As soon as Darby reached the trailhead, she searched the cluster of horses below. Although there were at least thirty horses crowded together, she picked out Hoku and Tango right away.

Weak with thankfulness, Darby leaned forward with her hands on her thighs. Then, she took a deep breath and started down the uneven path.

Even though it meant Cade caught up with her, Darby didn't run. Tripping would cost her more time than walking fast. Still, his expression was getting on her nerves. What in the world was he smiling about?

"Nice outfit," Cade said.

"Shut up," Darby requested. She glanced up from the rough footing at Cade. There wasn't much she could criticize about his clothes. He wore the same dark green poncho he always did.

Though he hadn't cracked a real smile, she could tell he was in a good mood. "Why are you so happy?"

"I'm not. Just glad no one's hurt bad," he said.

Darby matched Cade's steps, then noticed his blond braid. Most days, it was tucked up, out of sight. "Where's your hat?"

"Don't know." Cade clipped off the two words as if he didn't care, but Darby knew he did. Cade had told her he'd bought his hala hat with the very first paycheck he'd earned from Jonah. She was about to sympathize when he said, "Walk faster."

She did, but that meant ignoring her nightgown's tendency to come untucked. Instead of stopping to adjust it, Darby gave a huff of frustration.

The horses heard her. Although they were half a

mile away, two dozen concerned faces turned to see what was wrong.

"Don't spook 'em," Cade warned.

It was a definite possibility, Darby thought. Ninety-nine times out of a hundred, the horses were grazing when she looked at them. But not now.

Instead, they were milling together, still uneasy from the earthquake.

"You're the one carrying a rifle," Darby muttered. Her arms swung at her sides and she'd left her hands empty by tying Hoku's orange-and-white-striped lead rope around her waist.

"I wasn't talking about the rope. I meant your snorting."

Darby didn't reply. If she opened her mouth, she'd end up yelling at Cade and really scaring the horses.

Besides, he was probably only teasing her because he was relieved.

Aunty Cathy's reaction to the quake had been to kick the pumpkin can.

Kit had stood by, ready to tackle any job with his adrenaline buildup.

Jonah had shown unusual concern—for her and Megan, and for Aunty Cathy.

Darby shrugged. She guessed her own answer to being out of control of the world around her was to prove she could catch Hoku and bring back the saddle herd.

A blast of hot wind made the trees around her sway, and for a moment Darby felt dizzy again. It wouldn't hurt to show Jonah that falling off Navigator didn't mean she'd lost her touch with horses. But she'd better hurry up and do it, before a second earthquake or aftershock made Wild Horse Island sink back into the sea.

Cade looked pointedly at Darby's feet as if she'd been stomping as she walked.

"What?" she demanded quietly.

"I'm taking the rifle—"

"Did I ask?" Darby whispered.

"—because of what happened last time . . . "

". . . in the rain forest," Darby finished, admitting to herself that Cade's skill with a rifle had saved a rabid pig from suffering or hurting her horse, when Cade corrected her.

"No, the last time we had an earthquake," he said, but he didn't go on.

Cade was baiting her. If he was trying to make her beg to hear what had happened during the last earthquake, he had a long wait ahead of him.

Darby turned her attention back to the horses. They were much more interesting and Jonah was counting on her to bring them—or at least some of them—back to the main ranch. And she didn't know how much time she had before she'd have to start getting ready for school.

They looked like a wild herd, Darby thought.

Luna, the big bay Quarter Horse stallion, stood on a knoll, overlooking the mares, foals, and geldings, alert and on guard.

"Pigtail Fault," Cade said under his breath.

Darby couldn't help giving him a side glance.

"You haven't been up to Two Sisters yet, so you wouldn't know," he said, lording it over her. "But just as the ground really starts getting steep, there's a fracture in the earth—a fissure I guess they call it—and it slid open big enough that a herd of pigs, running from the quake, were jumping over it—"

"You saw this?" Darby asked.

"—and one didn't make it. He went head down into the crack—"

"I don't like this story," Darby said, picking up her pace.

"And then an aftershock came along," Cade said, bringing his hands together in a muffled clap. "And slammed the fissure closed. Left only the pig's tail sticking up."

"That's disgusting," Darby said.

"All the same, it happened," Cade said. "You'll see it—not the tail, but the crack—when you go up to the volcanoes."

"*Shh*," Darby hushed him.

Navigator, Conch, Biscuit, and Joker moved away from the other horses toward Darby and Cade. The horses moved side by side, a gaudy team suitable for a circus.

Look at them! Darby wanted to say, but she didn't want to spook the geldings. Their bay, grulla, buckskin, and Appaloosa coats caught the sun as they held their heads high. They studied Cade and Darby, weighing the safety of approaching even familiar humans on a day like this.

Kona, Jonah's big gray, started to follow them, but he stumbled. At the sound, the other geldings scattered. For a few seconds, Kona stopped, holding one hoof off the ground. But then Joker stood alone, frayed neck rope dangling, the only one that hadn't pivoted back toward the herd.

Just when Darby was telling herself she couldn't blame Cade because his horse loved him, Cade pretended not to notice. He was still talking about Pigtail whatever.

"And if you don't want to look, just ask Jonah."

"I will," Darby promised, though there'd be nothing left to prove it might be true.

Ten minutes later, Joker had ventured close enough to hear his master's voice.

"Here, brother."

The Appaloosa crossed the pasture, lowered his head, and all but begged for Cade's touch. Cade kept talking, persuading his horse to forget the earthquake.

"That's it, look at me." Cade extended his arm and caught a loose bridle rein. Joker took up the slack by moving a few steps away. "Around," Cade said, then made a clucking sound and Joker circled him at a walk.

Cade looked the gelding over for injuries, watching for pulled tendons or muscle damage as the horse moved.

Brother. Darby had never heard Cade call Joker by that nickname, and she admitted, but only to herself, that she envied the two.

During their best moments, she thought of Hoku as her sister, but she and the filly had a long way to go before they had the kind of relationship she saw before her.

"Halt," Cade said.

Joker did. Cade stepped close enough to push aside the gelding's black mane and stroke his crest. Joker closed his eyes, and Darby gasped.

"He'll be fine," Cade assured her, preparing to mount bareback.

"Don't rope anything," Darby said. "It'll hurt Joker's neck."

Cade stared at her. "Where'd you come up with that?"

"Won't it? I mean, it's pretty basic physiology," Darby told him, but the truth was, well, hard to believe.

"I guess," Cade said, sounding a little insulted.

He threw himself at Joker's back, then swung his legs up to fork the gelding. His hands rested on Joker's withers, waiting.

In the minutes Cade stayed quiet, letting Joker

settle down, Darby tried to analyze what had just passed between her and the Appaloosa.

When Joker had closed his freckled eyelids, she'd seen them twitch, showing the soreness under his mane, beneath Cade's hand.

Anyone could have guessed that, but muscles had actually stiffened in her own neck. She'd felt dizzy as she imagined a taut lariat running away from her. The whine of tightening rope fibers filled her ears, and she winced, afraid the impact of the horse's weight would wrench her neck.

His neck, she corrected herself.

After about five minutes, Joker's head drooped a few inches. He shifted his weight off a rear hoof and blew through his lips.

The Appaloosa had gotten over his scare. Darby wasn't so sure about herself.

Cade leaned forward, patted his horse's shoulder, then shot Darby a look of puzzled respect.

"We'll be careful," Cade said.

"Sure," Darby said. She lifted one shoulder as if his promise was no big deal, then turned her attention to the other horses, hoping they wouldn't follow the bouncing spots on the Appaloosa's hindquarters.

They didn't, but she was still left with the problem of catching Hoku. And, wait, if the other horses hadn't followed Joker, why should she believe they'd follow her filly?

Darby shrugged. It didn't matter what she

thought. Jonah thought they'd follow Hoku, so she'd give it a try.

She walked closer to the horses. They all watched her, Hoku most of all.

Darby stopped when Lady Wong and Blue Ginger snapped at their babies, making them back away from Darby instead of going to her as they usually did. The other horses swept their heads from side to side, looking somehow embarrassed as they backed away, too.

Only Tango remained beside Hoku. The rose roan mustang fretted and stamped, but she stayed, watching Hoku dip her head like a swan, before raising her muzzle to point at Darby. Hoku arched her golden neck again and repeated the movements, using her chin to draw long ovals in the air.

It almost looked like a dance.

"What's that, pretty girl?" Darby asked as she took a step closer.

In a tangle of legs and switching tails, the other horses scattered.

"You guys," Darby scoffed softly, "don't roll your eyes like you don't see me every day. I know the earthquake was scary, but I didn't do it."

Darby knew she couldn't just walk right up to Hoku and slip the rope around her neck. The rest of the horses acted like they were about to stampede. This wasn't going to work, but she had an idea of something else that might.

Darby looked back over her shoulder. She didn't see Jonah standing on the lanai or the cliff, looking down to make sure she didn't do anything dangerous. That was a good thing, too, because what she wanted to try was a little risky.

She sat down cross-legged in the middle of the pasture and pretended to be fascinated by her own hands. She only remembered a couple of finger games from her childhood.

Putting the knuckles of each hand together, she whispered, "Here's the church. . . ."

Interlacing her fingers, she pointed her index fingers up, tips touching.

"Here's the steeple. . . ."

She let her thumbs escape, pressed them side to side, then pulled them apart.

"Open the doors. . . ."

Darby lifted her eyelashes a fraction of a millimeter to see all the horses were watching her.

But then she turned her hands, fingers laced, upside down, and wiggled them wildly as she said, "And see all the people!"

Kōko and her silver-maned colt bolted. Luna pawed impatiently.

"I'm not leaving," Darby told him. At the same time, Hoku looked back at the big bay stallion and shivered her skin, as if his stare was a pesky insect crawling on her.

This little piggy went to market. This little— Wait.

That was a toe game you played with babies. Not that the horses would know the difference.

Darby didn't look up again until she heard teeth clipping grass.

The horses were relaxing. At least, Judge was. Darby dared to look up again and saw that the old horse had been joined by the brown bird that rode on his withers. The bird flared its wings to show white bars against the brown, then returned to harvesting minuscule bugs from the gelding's back.

Darby smiled as four horses eased away from the herd. Navigator, Judge, Tango, and Hoku grazed in her direction. Slowly, so slowly, but it was progress and she was excited. Until Luna decided to round them up.

At least, that's what she thought he was doing at first.

As Luna pranced toward the group of four, Tango and Hoku flattened their ears, but the geldings moved out of his path. The king was coming and they would not block him.

Hoku did. She stood beside Tango, but Luna looked past her, regarding Tango as if he'd never seen her before.

Luna reared. His arched neck shone like mahogany and his forelegs curved. His display was enough to send the walking geldings into a trot, leaving him with the two fillies.

Luna tucked his chin and gave a snort so loud it

made Darby jump. He was showing off, and he looked great doing it, Darby thought.

Tango's ears flattened, but the big bay didn't take the hint. He kept jogging forward.

Tango's eyes narrowed and even though her hooves didn't change position, she bared her teeth and her pink head snapped out like a snake's.

Not so impressed, Darby thought.

Luna strode on toward the fillies, planting each hoof with determination. He looked pretty serious about teaching Hoku and Tango a lesson in obedience.

But the two fillies had lived in the wild. They stood firm, guarding each other.

If some flip of forelock or widening of eyes signaled their defiance, Darby missed it.

Hoku charged past Luna. Maybe she was trying to lead him away, but the stallion rushed to Tango.

Whirling around, Hoku moved into position to kick Luna.

But the stallion had eyes in the back of his head, or he heard what Hoku was doing, because, instead of touching noses with Tango, he lashed out his own hind legs at the same time as Hoku.

Neither connected, so the moves were just warnings, but Darby bolted to her feet, afraid for either horse to be hurt.

"Stop it!" she yelled. "Luna!"

Darby waved her arms, hoping to distract the

horses, but she might as well have been mute and invisible.

This was bad. Luna outweighed Hoku by hundreds of pounds. If his sledgehammer hooves landed, they could break her slim legs.

Why would Luna fight a filly he'd been courting just last week?

Was it because Hoku was what Jonah had called a tomboy mare? The mustang filly had challenged two stallions: Luna and Black Lava.

Now, Luna reared and kicked out once more, then screamed his dominance.

Hoku sprinted away, but just when Darby's shoulders sagged in relief, she realized Hoku wasn't fleeing. She was galloping a protective circle around Tango.

The fillies made a game of their defiance. Heads tossing and eyes sparkling, they taunted the stallion.

But what if the stallion decided to discipline them?

He didn't. Luna gave a snort that might have meant disgust or amusement. Then he shook his mane and jogged back to his knoll.

When Darby realized both hands were flattened over her heart, she forced her arms to hang loose at her sides. Then she cleared her throat and whispered, "That could have been worse."

With both fillies safe from their own mischief, Darby smiled.

Watching the horses communicate had been fascinating. Of course she'd missed much of what was going on. It was like watching a play performed in another language. She'd understood enough to follow the basic plot.

I could watch wild animals for a living, Darby thought. Biologists and naturalists and all kinds of scientists did it.

So pay closer attention in science classes, she scolded herself. Like Ecology.

She still didn't know how she'd managed to forget a major assignment. It just wasn't like her!

Losing track of time wasn't like her, either, and she must have done precisely that, because now Jonah was watching her from the bluff.

"Expecting me to return at the head of a line of horses," Darby grumbled to herself. And that wasn't going to happen. Although, maybe . . .

She had one thing left to try. And it wouldn't work while Hoku and Tango faced away from her, nosing each other in congratulations over Luna's retreat.

But horses' eyes were on the sides of their heads. They had great peripheral vision, right?

"C'mon, Hoku," Darby whispered. She tightened her ponytail. "Hoku, my sweet, strong girl, you showed Luna who's boss. Now, come show me you're my friend."

Hoku's head swung around and she stared at

Darby. Hoku took deep breaths, and with each one her head rose higher. She knew Darby had freed her from the corral. Maybe that comforted her enough to return, because Hoku danced on nervous hooves toward Darby, circling her as she had Tango.

"That's my beauty," Darby said. "You are such a smart girl. You know I didn't cause all that shaking, don't you? And I let you run when you felt like you had to get away from it."

Good thing no humans stood near enough to hear, Darby thought. Her gushing sounded crazy, or at least peculiar.

"Abnormal." Darby pronounced the word with exaggerated precision and Hoku shook her head, making a blizzard of her blond forelock in front of her eyes. She looked like she was laughing, and when Darby started walking, Hoku followed her without the lead rope looped around her neck.

A deep neigh made Darby turn.

Luna gazed toward Sun House. He'd spotted Jonah. With no more than a snap of his fingers, her grandfather could probably call the bay stallion to him. But he wouldn't.

The man and the stallion had an understanding. Luna guarded the mares and foals while Jonah ran things up at the ranch.

Darby had climbed halfway back to Sun House, when she heard the rasp of more hooves. She glanced back to see Navigator and Biscuit pass Hoku. Then they were right behind her, and after giving her hair a sniff, the two geldings paced ahead, returning to their home and hay.

They trust me, Darby thought.

Without meaning to, she walked a little taller, but when she reached the top of the path, Hoku stopped.

The filly glanced right, looking down the driveway as it became a street to the highway. She looked left, at the two geldings, Jonah, and her corral. Then the filly swerved toward Darby, but questions clouded her eyes.

"C'mon, girl," Darby whispered. "It'll be okay."

Would it? Darby wondered. What if there was an aftershock while she was at school? Cade was gone, Aunty Cathy might go to the doctor, and Kimo was already later than usual. Kit was under his house, assessing damage, and Jonah was now squatted there, too, talking to him.

Darby turned cold, thinking how helpless they'd be if there was another serious quake.

She looked back at her horse and wondered. Would anyone think of freeing Hoku from her corral a second time?

Darby couldn't promise her horse safety, and Hoku sensed it, turning her gaze back to the pasture.

"I understand," Darby told Hoku. Then, even though she dreaded trying to explain this silent conversation to Jonah, Darby made a vague shooing motion to let the sorrel know she was free to go.

Lady Wong uttered a whinny, stretching her long, gray neck in a way that made it seem as if she was calling Hoku.

The filly stood so close, Darby could have swung the lead rope around her neck, or touched the white star on her sorrel chest.

"I think you're better off down there for now, but you'd better remember this when I come to get you after school," Darby warned.

Hoku made no promises. She simply wheeled on her back hooves and galloped down the trail, before Darby changed her mind.

Chapter 6

Darby expected Jonah to be angry.

What do you have to say for yourself? he'd probably demand.

So Darby prepared excuses as she walked.

She hadn't caught Hoku, but she had gotten him a horse—a choice of two, actually—to ride to Tutu's cottage.

Besides, she'd *allowed* Hoku to go. It had been her decision, not the filly's. And Jonah always claimed he wouldn't second-guess her when it came to Hoku.

But it turned out her excuses weren't necessary.

Maybe the earthquake had shaken a little sarcasm out of her grandfather, Darby thought.

As they met in front of Sun House, Jonah only

said, "You open the cage and a wild bird will fly out."

"I let her go, after she came to me."

"I saw." Jonah nodded, looking weary. The hair at his temples looked grayer than usual.

"Hoku would have come all the way back up here, if I'd asked her to," Darby said. When Jonah gave a skeptical smile, she insisted, "Really, she would have."

"If you say so." Jonah yawned, then pointed at his brown Land Rover. "Looks like Megan's ready to go."

Alarm crackled through Darby. Megan. School. Aunty Cathy. And she still hadn't called her mom. How could her mind have floated so far away?

Aunty Cathy was walking toward the truck, so Darby waved and hurried up to her.

"How do you feel?" Darby asked first.

"Okay," Aunty Cathy said, then admitted, "A little weird. Kind of like I'm looking at things from a distance." Hearing what she'd said, she amended, "I'm fine to drive, but I think I'll take Jonah's advice and stop by the doctor's office, just to be—Darby, what are you doing?"

Darby had been standing on tiptoe, trying to see past Aunty Cathy's messy brown-blond bangs, but she hadn't meant to be obvious. "I was checking to see if your pupils were both the same size. I've read that when people get head injuries, that's one of the first things you're supposed to do."

Aunty Cathy squeezed Darby in a one-armed

hug, then opened her eyes wide, and let Darby look.

"They seem the same," Darby told her.

"Thanks, honey," Aunty Cathy said, then glanced at her watch.

Darby said quickly, "I'll be right back, after I call my mom—"

"The power's out and the phone lines are down, even in Hapuna," Cathy said sympathetically.

Darby sighed. Her mom would understand.

"I'll just get my stuff, then."

And put on clothes, brush my hair, and grab some food, she added to herself, but when Aunty Cathy opened the Land Rover's door and made a sound of admiration, Darby stopped.

Hands on her hips, Cathy looked at the clean upholstery and dashboard smelling of coconut polish and mused, "Don't rush. This appears to be the one place on the ranch I won't have to clean up. Take your time and let me enjoy it."

Just the same, Darby sprinted toward the house.

"This was smart," Megan said to Darby as they walked onto the campus of Lehua High School.

"What was?"

"Starting with Nutrition Break instead of first-period classes," Megan said, waving as she glimpsed her friend Elane. "We can find out what's up with everybody—"

"And eat."

Megan saluted Darby's firm tone.

"I'm starving," Darby explained. "I bet it's some kind of survival response, so you'll be strong after an emergency and—"

"You could have eaten at home. I mean, there was food all over the place," Megan teased.

"I know. Do you hear that?" Darby asked, looking down at the gummy sound of each step she took. "I think my soles are coated with pineapple juice."

As her stomach growled, she mentally thanked Aunty Cathy for reaching into the ranch cash box to give her and Megan enough money to buy food at the snack carts.

Most students had been shaken from bed by the earthquake and many of them had been awake ever since, but you wouldn't know it, Darby thought, by the noisy chatter as they waited in line for food.

Darby had just noticed that her cousin Duckie stood at the front of the line, already chugging milk, when an arm reached out to grab Megan's elbow.

"I saved you a place," Elane said, dragging Megan into line.

Darby flashed a sheepish look at the guy they'd just cut in front of and asked, "Is it okay?"

Shoulders hunched, hands shoved deep in the pockets of baggy shorts, the guy looked like he was asleep on his feet.

Darby smiled at his black hair, rumpled into something like a cockatoo's crest. In slow motion, he looked up, blinked as if she'd wakened him, and gave a "be my guest" wave of his hand, so Darby tucked in behind Megan.

" . . . almost six point zero on the Richter scale," Elane was saying. "Centered on the Big Island, near Hilo, and why do I know that? Oh yeah, you remember how much my mom and dad laughed when I spent all my summer job money on a special cabinet with baby-safe locks for my computer? Turns out they're earthquake-proof, too, and my computer's not facedown with a cracked screen like the television."

Elane looked pleasantly smug, Darby thought. The girl, with her short brown hair and glasses, loved her computer. She was so skilled, teachers consulted her all the time for troubleshooting.

"Hey dude, howzit!"

"Hey! Bet you was scared?"

"Nah . . ."

Darby didn't look back, but she was pretty sure the denial came from the cockatoo-crested boy who was in line behind her. He and another guy must be doing some friendly scuffling, too, she thought, because one of them bumped her shoulder.

"No shame, you can tell me."

"Nah, I went back to bed. That's why I'm so messed up!"

Darby sneaked a glance over her shoulder to see the cockatoo guy tousling his own hair, making it even worse, as he talked. She was returning his grin when his friend, a guy in a gray hooded sweatshirt, wheeled on her, sneering, then turned back to his friend.

"Haole girl's givin' you the stink eye!" he hooted.

"I am not!" Darby snapped, but just then Megan jiggled her shoulder.

"Order," Megan said.

"Really, I wasn't," Darby said, still looking back at the boys. Despite her protest, the guy in gray was still doubled up, laughing at his friend and pointing at Darby.

"Haole crab!"

Darby couldn't tell which of the boys had said it, but Megan was not pleased.

"Come on!" Megan raised her voice to Darby, gestured toward the snack-cart lady, then turned on the two guys and barked a few words Darby couldn't understand.

Darby wasn't nearly as hungry as she'd been a couple of minutes ago, especially when she realized that the guy in the hood was in one of her classes.

"What did you say to them?" Darby asked Megan.

"Never mind," Megan said, hiding a smile behind her breakfast wrap of Spam and eggs. "There are a few Hawaiian phrases you'll have to learn on your own. And that was one of them."

Miss Day's English class was a madhouse. Darby noticed that at the same time she saw her friend Ann's seat was empty.

Darby was looking around, searching for Ann amid all the students gathered in the back of the classroom or between the rows of desks, when Miss Day bustled in.

The teacher almost immediately decided to give in to a period of noisy conversation.

Calling it a lesson in oral expression, Miss Day went around the room, asking students to describe their earthquake morning.

A few students were more nervous about what would happen next than what had already happened. Some repeated their parents' stories about earthquakes, volcanic eruptions, and tsunamis of the past that had begun just like this, while others argued over conflicting radio or TV reports about the quake's magnitude.

Monica Waipunalei, a girl Darby knew from P.E., said an earthen dam had broken above her house and filled the subdivision she lived in with slimy chocolate-colored water.

Cheryl Hong, another girl from P.E., said her brother had gotten up early to work on his car and his arm had been broken when the car fell off the jack, pinning him there until two neighbors lifted it off him.

Darby kept glancing at the clock, hoping Ann was safe. And she kept thinking about the guy in the gray sweatshirt. *Haole girl's givin' you the stink eye,* he'd said. But she hadn't given him a dirty look. And did she qualify as a haole if she was one-quarter Hawaiian?

Never mind, she told herself.

Then, because her turn was coming and she didn't know what to say, Darby listened uneasily to Morris, a guy who reveled in being the class clown as he confided that his pet mynah bird had screeched "Nevermore!" all night.

Darby was rubbing superstitious chills from her arms when Morris added, "Of course, my mynah only knows three words, and *nevermore* is the only one we can understand."

As the class's laughter subsided, Darby decided to tell about last night's dog howls and Navigator's bucking.

"I don't know that much about it, but I've heard animals can kind of predict earthquakes," she finished.

"You should ask Mr. Silva about that," Miss Day told her.

"I will," Darby said, but she was glad three other students began arguing whether or not such a thing could be true, and if it was, should it be attributed to the animals' instincts or physical sensitivity.

Mr. Silva was her Ecology teacher. In his billowing white lab coat and shoulder-length, gray-streaked black hair, Mr. Silva looked like he should be teaching wizardry rather than science. He was one of Darby's favorite teachers ever, but her stomach hurt when she imagined his reaction to her missing home-work.

Darby was picturing herself walking into Ecology to see ALL HOMEWORK DEADLINES EXTENDED BECAUSE OF EARTHQUAKE written on the board. That way Mr. Silva wouldn't know she'd messed up.

Just then, the bell to end class rang, and Ann Potter popped through the door.

Ann was greeted with a spontaneous round of applause. Darby smiled. Apparently she wasn't the only one who'd noticed Ann's absence and was worried about her.

Blushing so that her freckles stood out even more than usual, Ann patted her red hair as if she could subdue the curls into order, and then she bowed.

Because Darby and Ann had their first three classes together, by the time they reached Ecology, Darby had managed to tell Ann about her adventure in set-ting Hoku free, then rounding her up, about Aunty Cathy's accident, and about Megan's crack-the-whip episode with Francie the fainting goat.

But she hadn't told Ann that she'd forgotten to interview Tutu. She just didn't know how to say it, especially since Ann seemed a little, well, spacey as she talked about the strange pre-earthquake behavior of the Potters' horses.

"Soda, who's never cribbed before, was eating wood like a termite. So, yeah . . ." Ann's voice trailed off as if something worse had happened.

Darby hated the idea of making a bad day worse for her friend. She found herself depending on her daydream that Mr. Silva would put off the assignment.

"It was just a little teeny fire," Ann explained as they walked toward Lehua High's science wing, "from an electrical short, I think, so . . ."

"A fire?" Darby yelped, and her reaction worked on Ann like a bucket of cold water.

"Really, it was just a little flare-up. Moving the horses was a precaution. Of course we wanted to get all of them out of the barn, anyway, but they wouldn't go!"

"Not even Sugarfoot?" Darby asked. Although she hadn't met Ann's caramel-and-white pinto, she couldn't believe he wouldn't follow Ann out of a burning barn.

"Nope," Ann said.

"I've heard of that before—"

"Of horses being stupid? Yeah, me too."

The voice that interrupted belonged to Darby's cousin Duxelles Borden—nicknamed Duckie by Darby.

The big girl shortened her strides to walk next to Darby for a few steps and Darby wondered if she'd ever get used to Duckie's appearance. A sheet of metal-bright blond hair fell to her shoulders. The hem of her denim skirt was about five feet off the ground and though her white blouse might have looked Victorian on some girls, the size of Duckie's biceps made her look, well, not so demure.

I'll stick with my first impression, Darby thought as her cousin strode past. *Duckie looks like a Viking.*

"Anyhow," Darby said, shaking her head to dispel the image of her cousin, "I don't get why horses do that."

She was stalling, making Ann linger outside the door of their Ecology class, because what if Mr. Silva hadn't postponed the assignment? Ann didn't seem to mind. In fact, despite the hot wind that whipped hair into their faces, Ann seemed no more eager to go inside than Darby.

"My mom says it's because the horses think they're safe at home, but my dad sees it a little differently," Ann said. "He says it's a choice between 'the devil you know and the devil you don't know.'"

Darby tried to puzzle that out.

"I guess no matter how bad it is in the stall with a fire burning toward them, they still think it might be better than what's on the other side of the door," Ann explained.

Darby looked at the classroom door. Ann had given her the perfect opening to admit what she'd done.

"Speaking of . . ." But Darby couldn't make the confession. "I mean, that's not true for all horses, is it?"

"Well, this is the first barn fire I've ever seen,"

Ann admitted, as two girls, almost late for class, slipped past them, "but I think—no. You've got to remember that most of our horses are rescues. They've had bad experiences with people. But if the horse really trusted you—like Hoku does you—I think it would know you wouldn't make it walk through fire!"

Chapter 7

"Pop quiz, pupils!" Mr. Silva was flapping around in his white lab coat when Darby and Ann came into class.

The bell still echoed inside the classroom, but Mr. Silva was wasting no time.

Darby stared at the blank board. How could Mr. Silva do this to her? And then his words registered.

"Pop quiz?" Darby's whisper joined a student chorus of horror.

"The delayed start gave you two extra hours to study. Or sleep." Mr. Silva pointed his index finger and swept it from one side of the classroom all the way to the other. "Judging by the fifty percent of you who didn't turn in your online homework, and my nearly empty in-basket, I'd say it was the latter."

"It's not bad enough we nearly died in an earthquake?" Ann moaned.

"Miss Potter, feel free to elaborate on your near-death experience in the essay portion of the quiz," Mr. Silva said. He paused a minute, looking from Ann to Darby and back to Ann, before handing her a stack of papers to pass back. "I must say I'm surprised at your lack of concern for your team project."

When the science teacher strode to the next row, the girls faced each other.

Certain she'd turned gray with guilt, Darby blurted, "I can explain—"

Ann said, "Here's the thing—"

Darby felt dizzy with blame, but Mr. Silva interrupted before she could finish her confession.

"No talking during the quiz," he commanded.

Ann didn't say another word. Just the same, while Darby worked on her quiz, she felt Ann's lingering glare.

The quiz on volcanoes included two extra-credit questions about the epicenter and Richter scale measurement of this morning's earthquake. If the radio report and Megan's friend Elane had been right, Darby was, too. And she could use those extra-credit points.

Once she finished, Darby turned her quiz facedown, but she didn't look at Ann. Instead, she used her fingertip to draw an invisible, endless spiral on her desktop.

"All is not lost," Mr. Silva said as he collected the quiz papers. "Given this morning's extraordinary circumstances, those students who handed in their work on time will receive bonus points —"

"Oh yeah!" someone cheered.

" — and the rest of you will still be eligible for full credit if — listen, please! Don't celebrate yet, because this next part is crucial. You will only be eligible for full credit if you turn in A-quality work."

Darby sprawled back in her desk and looked toward the ceiling with thanks. She couldn't help noticing Ann had slumped forward at the same time.

"Working toward that end, we'll spend the rest of the class period discussing questions that might come up on your projects during spring break."

As Mr. Silva spoke, Darby tried to make her brain a thirsty sponge. She understood about searching out parallels between stories and science. She got the part about observation and field notes, too, but Megan had told her that the Two Sisters never did more than breathe out a few wisps of steam.

"Mr. Silva?" Darby edged her hand up, barely even with her head. "What if our project is something we can't observe?"

"I'm sure you'll think of something. That's why it's a vacation assignment. So you'll have plenty of time."

Darby heard a few students grumble about Mr. Silva's misunderstanding of the word *vacation*, but most already looked thoughtful.

"Now take five minutes to sit quietly and make some notes. Then I'll call on a few of you, at random, to see if you're on the right track."

Darby whipped out a pen and paper. For a few seconds she stared at the light blue lines on the paper, waiting for something to materialize.

She heard students whispering to each other about Kane and Kanaloa, but she didn't know either of those names. Someone mentioned Maui the trickster, and a guy in the row next to her mentioned Mano. She thought that had something to do with sharks. She wrote down *menehune*, because she knew who they were, but she didn't know if they could be linked with volcanoes.

"Oh! Pele!" Darby didn't know excitement had made her blurt the words aloud until Ann smiled and other students giggled.

"Very good, Miss Carter," her teacher said. "Pele would tie in nicely with your project on volcanoes."

Darby was looking down, blushing even though she was right, when she heard a mocking snort from the back of the room.

"Shouldn't go mocking Pele, you know. She's one bad lady when she's mad."

Darby recognized the voice, and she'd already turned to see the guy in the gray hooded sweatshirt when Mr. Silva said, "Tyson, I'm sure Miss Carter means to do no such thing. . . ."

"I don't," Darby insisted, but just as he had earlier, the guy sneered as if she was lying.

"Since, unless I'm mistaken, she lives in Pele's backyard," Mr. Silva finished.

Darby gave a quick nod, looked down to avoid a few curious looks, and scribbled down the names Pele and Pigman and the word *fern*, and hoped she'd said enough that Mr. Silva wouldn't call on her.

She had. Even better, the bell rang, and she could finally explain things to Ann.

"I'm so sorry—" Darby began.

"I'm sorry! I didn't mean to fall asleep, but—"

"What?" Darby and Ann blurted the word together.

The corridor was filled with students and noise, but Darby felt her thoughts click into place as if she were surrounded by silence.

"You mean, you didn't do the experiment?" Darby asked.

"And you didn't do the interview?" Ann gasped.

"I thought we were such good students," Darby said, giving Ann a gentle elbow in her ribs.

"What a couple of slackers," Ann said, and then they were both laughing and making excuses.

"It was because Navigator was acting so weird, and then Jonah—"

"I know," Ann said. "And I was just going to sleep for a couple of hours and the next thing I knew I was getting tossed around like a frog in a blender. . . ."

"Yuck!" Darby shoved Ann down the hall and

she was about to dart off toward the gym and P.E., one of only two classes she didn't share with Ann, when something really unpleasant crossed her mind. "Hey, what's up with that kid Tyson?"

"Ty's not so bad, but . . ." Ann's red hair bounced as she shook her head.

"But what?" Darby asked.

"He's a little bit of a bully. He thought he might scare you with that crack about Pele."

"He called me a haole, too," Darby pointed out.

"That's not always bad," Ann said. "It depends on how he said it. I remember at my first rodeo here, I heard someone say, 'That haole girl barrel racer? She's pretty good.' And they were talking about me. Sometimes it's just descriptive."

"Tyson didn't say it in a good way, that's for sure. Besides, I'm not—" Darby broke off, shrugging. She wasn't comfortable talking about race. In Pacific Pinnacles, kids pretended to ignore ethnicity unless they were filling out some kind of form, or were racist.

"Probably you're a *hapa*-haole," Ann said in a consoling voice.

Half white, Darby defined the words for herself. That wasn't right, either. And Tyson's tone hadn't been descriptive, but sarcastic.

"See you in Algebra," Darby said with a wave.

Ann waved back and walked with a slight limp from her still-healing soccer injury in the direction of the office. Darby had veered toward the gym and was mulling over what Ann had said when Duckie appeared again, right in front of her.

With her feet slightly apart and hands out level with her shoulders, Darby's cousin blocked most of the hallway. She stood so close, Darby almost walked right into her. Now, looking up to see her cousin's face, Darby had a pretty good idea of how Jack felt when he got to the top of the beanstalk and encountered a giant.

"Hey!" Duckie said.

Darby glanced over her shoulder. Duckie rarely sounded so friendly except to other swimmers and rich kids. But as long as she was here, Darby couldn't resist asking, "Are you all okay, over at Sugar Sands Cove? Did any of the guests get hurt? What about the horses?" Darby's mental picture of Stormbird, the cute foal she'd helped rescue, wiped out most of her worry over the luxurious resort run by her aunt Babe.

"Things were kind of crazy, but we've got plenty of help."

"What about Stormbird?" Darby asked, even though Duckie gave an impatient roll of her eyes.

"He stayed with all those white horses."

Safety was with the herd, Darby thought. As she thought of Hoku standing up for Tango, Luna looking up at Jonah but not going to him, and Lady Wong calling Hoku back to the horses, she knew it was true.

Suddenly jittery to get back to the ranch and check on Hoku, Darby jumped when Duckie interrupted her thoughts.

"I'm going to give you some advice."

"Okay," Darby said carefully, though Duckie clearly wasn't waiting for permission.

"I saw Ty giving you some trouble."

"No big deal," Darby said, though she enjoyed a brief fantasy in which her cousin pinched Tyson's hood between two fingers and lifted him off the ground so that his legs pedaled in midair.

"It's because he doesn't know who you are," Duckie said.

"What do you mean?" Darby asked. "Of course he does. Mr. Silva calls me by name all the time."

Her cousin winced as if her stomach hurt. Then, in a tone indicating Darby wasn't very smart, she enunciated, "You need to find a group. You've been here two weeks, and what are you?"

"What am I?"

"Like jock, nerd, surfer, drama llama, you know." Duckie snapped her fingers right under Darby's nose. "Your clique."

Clique?

Darby could tell Duckie thought she was doing her a huge favor, so she tried to sound nice as she explained, "I usually just have one or two friends. Like Ann and Megan. . . ."

Should she add "and you"? Darby had no idea.

As she fumbled for what to say next, Duckie made a sound of frustration.

"You don't get it. They're in groups." Frowning in concentration, Duckie bent her neck to one side until it made a cracking sound. Apparently satisfied, she went on. "They're both jocks. Ann's part of that artsy crowd, too."

Darby thought a minute. If Megan had been offering her these recommendations, she might have given them serious consideration. But it felt weird getting advice from Duckie.

Still, since Duckie was pretty much a bully herself, she might know how Tyson thought. And Duckie hadn't been at Lehua High long, either. Her advice could be sincere.

"Is there a horse group?" Darby ventured.

"Are you crazy?" Duckie demanded.

Darby guessed that meant no.

"You passed up being a jock," Duckie said, "and don't think I don't appreciate it!" Duckie gave Darby an openhanded pat on the shoulder for not joining the swim team, because they both excelled in water sports, but Darby excelled just a little bit more. "I guess you could be a nerd," Duckie said as she studied Darby. "You're not even a freshman, so you can't be on the newspaper or yearbook."

"Thanks," Darby said. "I really appreciate—"

Duckie loomed over her cousin as she added, "You don't want to end up hanging out with those losers that smoke behind the bleachers. The Outsiders, they call themselves," Duckie said in a mocking tone.

How could outsiders have a group? Darby took a breath to tell Duckie that didn't make sense, but she was pretty sure her cousin didn't want to hear logic, especially while she was trying to be nice.

Besides, Duckie had stopped just short of the locker room door to tense her arm and feel one of her own muscles. On a horse, that muscle would be her withers. Darby didn't know what it was called on a human, but Duckie squeezed it with grave satisfaction.

Considering Duckie and horses in the same thought led Darby to wonder if Duckie was saying safety was with the herd.

"What?" Duckie asked, when she finally felt Darby watching.

"It's just . . . ," Darby began. She looked into her cousin's broad, rosy face and felt torn. She was grateful for Duckie's advice. But she didn't believe it. At least not for humans. "I kind of think all the groups are connected."

Even though her cousin made a sound sort of like a bull, Darby would have explained, if Duckie hadn't propelled her into the locker room with a push between her shoulder blades.

"I don't know why I waste my time on you," Duckie muttered.

* * *

By the time P.E. ended and Darby slipped into her desk in Algebra, she couldn't contain her eagerness to see Hoku.

"Are you dying to see your horses?" she asked Ann.

"Absolutely," Ann said. "I really need to work with Sugarfoot."

"When do I get to meet him?" Darby pretended to whine.

"Not until our camping trip," Ann said, but then she asked, "Jonah's still cool with it, isn't he?"

"I think so. It's for a school assignment."

"I just thought he might worry that the volcanoes would get restless," Ann explained.

"He didn't say anything."

Ann rolled her eyes.

"Yeah, he might have had a few other things on his mind," Darby admitted, but Jonah had been nice this morning, since the earthquake. Almost as if he'd never said *Granddaughter, I wash my hands of you.*

And yet, he hadn't apologized, either.

"Coach Roffmore sure is late," Darby said, glancing at the clock.

Ann shrugged, then asked, "Do you still want to take Hoku? From what you've told me, she's pretty green, and it's probably just a story, but some people say there are wild horses up there."

"Yeah," Darby said. "But if there's another earthquake, she's got to be with me."

And I've got to be with her, Darby thought.

Just then a rustle went through the classroom and a man—who wasn't Coach Roffmore—came through the door.

He announced that he was the coach's substitute, then started writing a huge Algebra assignment on the board.

Ann's hand shot up as soon as he'd finished.

"Can we please work in partners?" Ann asked, and Darby wondered how her friend managed to say it and still sound seriously studious.

The sub looked dubious, but he agreed.

Since Duckie wasn't likely to hear her over the screech of desks being moved every which way, Darby confided her conversation with her cousin to Ann.

"So what do you think?" she asked finally.

"I don't pay much attention to cliques," Ann said. Then, opening her Algebra book, Ann touched an example in her book and looked expectantly at Darby. "What I think is, we should make a list of what food we'll each bring for our trip, while we look totally mathematical."

"Great idea," Darby said, then whispered, "I guess I shouldn't be taking social guidance from Duckie too seriously."

"Hey, Cousin!"

Darby tried not to cringe as she swiveled in her desk, looking back at Duckie. She couldn't possibly have heard.

No way.

Could she?

"Yes?" Darby hissed as if everyone else in the room wasn't already listening.

"Just remember, people who live in grass houses shouldn't throw stones."

Darby formed an "okay" sign with her fingers and gave a weak smile. If she had any idea what Duckie was talking about she'd know whether to be amused or afraid.

Chapter 8

"Did Mr. Silva give you an F?" Megan asked.

Since Miss Day had canceled soccer practice, they walked out of school together.

"No. But I have to get an A on that part of the project when we turn it in after break," Darby said.

"Were you the only one who didn't do it?" Megan asked.

"No, even—" Darby had been about to tell Megan that even Ann hadn't done her part, but she just said, "Lots of people were going to do it this morning and they couldn't because of the earth-quake."

"So why are you, like, hanging your head?" Megan asked.

Darby hadn't realized she was, but Megan was probably right. She wasn't used to being an irresponsible student, and the mistake had been bothering her all day.

"I guess school is harder here than it was . . ." Darby hesitated. She'd been about to say "back home," but she couldn't. Every day, 'Iolani Ranch felt more like her real home.

"Or maybe you've got a life outside school," Megan said. "It's easy for nerds to get good grades, because all they do is study. No offense, because I know you used to be one, but it's a lot bigger accomplishment if you get good grades when you're doing chores, training horses—"

"And playing soccer," Darby put in.

"I was talking about you, not me."

"Maybe," Darby said, but she was thinking that Megan—by talking about nerds—had slipped into that same categorizing thing that Duckie had done.

While they waited in front of the school for a ride home, Darby started to feel anxious about getting back to the ranch. She barely heard Megan talking about her excitement over the camping trip. "It used to be so much fun to lead the Boy Scouts through the lava tube with my dad," Megan was saying, but Darby couldn't concentrate on anything but her horse.

"Do you think Hoku stayed with the other horses?" she interrupted.

Megan looked a little miffed.

"Sorry," Darby said, but Megan understood her worry.

"She was pretty scared, but there are older horses out there, which must be comforting to her."

Darby nodded, picturing Hoku rubbing noses over her corral fence with Judge and the way, just yesterday, that Hoku had ignored the strangeness of the round pen to coax Navigator into some social scratching.

"Here comes Kimo!" Megan shrugged out of her backpack as the faded maroon Ram Charger swooped in to pick them up.

"Hey, girls." Kimo leaned down to peer through the passenger-side window, then leaned across to open the door decorated with the 'Iolani Ranch owl, so that they could climb in. "Been waitin' long?"

Megan slid in first, and Darby was surprised when she kissed Kimo on each cheek, until she remembered that was exactly how Kimo had greeted her at the Hapuna Airport.

"Everything's okay over at your place, then?" Megan asked as she fastened her seat belt, then cleared a clutter of CDs off the seat so that Darby could settle in.

"A few things cracked and snapped," Kimo said, steering them back to the highway. "Mother Nature just helpin' us with housekeeping."

Megan sucked in a breath. "I never thought of

that. Wow, I hope my mom stayed out of my stuff. She's always saying, 'That's got to go.' This could be her big excuse to throw things away."

"So hey," Kimo said, glancing at Darby. "When you two going *holoholo* with crazy Ann?"

Going holoholo meant "taking a pleasure trip," so Darby pretended to be insulted.

"We're going on our research trip."

"Monday morning, early," Megan told him. "The Potters are bringing a horse van to take us partway." Megan danced to imaginary music, despite her seat belt and cramped position. Then she turned to Darby. "This is going to be so cool. And you'll like Ann's parents."

"Good people," Kimo agreed.

"I bet they are," Darby said, but she still felt a little shy about meeting them.

Besides helping with the Ecology project, Ann's dad had offered to start picking Darby up after school when he picked up Ann, on days that Megan had soccer practice. That way Darby could get right to the ranch.

Apparently the music in Megan's head had come to an end, because she slouched back against her seat. After a few minutes, she turned to Kimo.

"You know who Darby met today? One of your neighbors."

Was she talking about Tyson? Darby gave Megan a warning poke with her elbow.

"Ty?" Kimo asked. "He's not a bad kid, but . . ."

"You're the third person who's said that!" Darby told him.

"Said . . . ?" Kimo glanced away from the road at Darby.

"'Tyson's not a bad kid, *but* . . .'"

"Mo bettah I say *however*?" Kimo asked, straight-faced.

Darby laughed, then settled back in her seat. She hoped it was the end of the conversation. Megan had already made it too much of a big deal by yelling at the guy that morning.

But still she couldn't let it go.

"He called her a haole crab," Megan said.

Kimo made a disgusted sound.

"How bad is that?" Darby asked.

"Depends," Kimo said. "There is such a thing, you know, a white crab. But Ty's just got no sense. His parents are afraid he's gonna get hurt."

"He's ambushing people all the time," Megan explained to Darby. "Tourists who go hiking down into the valley or snorkling in *kapu* places."

"Forbidden?" Darby asked.

"Not really," Kimo told her. "Just off-limits, because he and his friends like to surf there."

That didn't sound so bad, Darby thought. The guy hiding inside his gray hoodie was probably just playacting at being tough.

They rode along in silence for a few minutes

until Kimo said, "He doesn't bother girls. Does he, Mekana?"

Kimo was one of the few people Megan allowed to call her by her Hawaiian name.

"Why are you asking me?" Megan shrugged as she twisted her long reddish-black hair up off her neck, holding it there so she wouldn't be so hot.

"He don't," Kimo said emphatically, then reached over and gave Darby's leg the same kind of pat he'd give a nine-hundred-pound horse. "You got nothin' to worry about."

Darby was leaning forward against her seat belt, eager to see Hoku, when she spotted the tan Land Rover ahead of them.

"Is that Jonah's truck?"

"Yeah," Kimo said. He glanced nervously at Megan.

"What's wrong?" she asked. "Is it Mom?"

For a few seconds, Darby could have sworn she heard Megan's heart beating, but then she realized it was her own.

"Jonah bullied her into seeing the doctor. 'Bout had to hog-tie her to get her loaded up." Kimo's forced humor didn't stop Megan from turning pale. She released her hold on her hair and it tumbled down over her shoulders as she said, "Drive faster. Please."

Kimo didn't argue, but he accelerated only a little bit. His eyes met Darby's and he seemed to be asking her to do something to calm Megan's fear.

"It can't be that bad," Darby said, leaning her shoulder against her friend's. "She just got hit by a can of pumpkin."

"Yeah, and my dad just fell off a horse."

Darby flinched. How could she have been so stupid? Of course Megan was reacting strongly to her mother's trip to the doctor; her father had been dead only two years.

"I'm sorry," Darby said. Megan just shook her head, but as the Ram Charger clanged over the cattle guard and into the ranch yard, she reached over and squeezed Darby's hand.

As soon as Kimo pulled into the ranch driveway, Darby bailed out of the truck so that Megan wouldn't have to climb over her.

Before she saw her grandfather or Aunty Cathy, Darby heard them quarreling.

"Jonah, please move out of my way. No, you are not carrying me!" Aunty Cathy's blue shirt and brown-blond hair was just visible past Jonah, who helped her down from the truck.

Aunty Cathy had sidled away from Jonah, and began tucking her hair behind her ears, when Megan came at her.

"Mom!"

Closing her daughter in a hug, Aunty Cathy was quiet for a minute.

"Now you see?" Aunty Cathy demanded of

Jonah, but she said it quietly, and she was still patting Megan's back.

For an instant, Darby's heart contracted, missing her own mother, but then she moved closer to Aunty Cathy and asked, "What did the doctor say?"

"She said that I was lucky to get just a bump on the head when a dozen people on this island broke arms and legs," Aunty Cathy said pointedly.

Darby was pretty sure the sharp tone was aimed at Jonah, but he didn't take the hint.

"The doctor said Catherine must take it easy, but we can't let her sleep. We have to keep track of her level of consciousness—"

"Just as a precaution, and only for twenty-four hours—"

"But forty-eight hours would be better," Jonah insisted.

"Wait," Megan said, withdrawing from her mother's hug to ask. "Level of consciousness? What exactly does that mean?"

Aunty Cathy put off answering by leaning down to rumple Peach's ears. The Australian shepherd arranged himself over Aunty Cathy's shoes, announcing he was on guard.

"Mom?"

"It just means to make sure I'm not acting loony," Aunty Cathy explained, but she couldn't joke away Megan's concern.

"Why?" Megan turned to Jonah.

"She has a concussion and a bad headache," Jonah told her.

"Can't they give her pills for the pain?" Kimo's question surprised them all, but his expression said he wasn't about to go do chores until he was sure Cathy didn't need his help.

"No," Jonah said. "If the headache gets worse, it could mean she's bleeding inside her skull."

Megan moaned and Aunty Cathy glared at Jonah.

"Why did you have to say that?"

"Megan will be looking after you. She's old enough to be told the truth," Jonah said, and he didn't sound a bit sorry.

"Thanks," Megan said. Then she took a deep breath and said, "Come upstairs, Mom, and I'll make you some tea."

"Oh, for heaven's sake, Megan." Aunty Cathy sounded like she didn't know whether to laugh or cry.

Peach made a concerned yodeling sound, but he didn't move off her feet.

"She can have tea, can't she?" Megan asked, ignoring her mother's outburst.

"Sure," Jonah said.

"Excuse me, Peach," Aunty Cathy apologized as she displaced the dog.

Panting and wagging his tail uncertainly, Peach watched along with the rest of them as Megan prodded her mother up the stairs to their apartment.

"Yell if you need anything," Jonah called, and behind her mother's back, Megan's fingers made an "okay" sign.

Darby was kind of aware that Jonah was headed toward Sun House. She sort of noticed Peach, nudging her hand so she'd stroke his head. But her mind was spinning with dark possibilities.

Was everything okay? Jonah had approved the overnight trip to Two Sisters because he trusted Megan's skill on the volcanic slopes. Megan knew Two Sisters' beauties, dangers, and history.

Her grandfather said Megan was the best guide two mainland girls like Ann and Darby could have.

Without meaning to, Darby counted the hours Megan had to sit at her mother's bedside. Twenty-four or forty-eight, Jonah had said. Today was Friday. The Potters would arrive with the horse van on Monday. None of their plans had to change.

Trying not to worry, Darby shrugged and scuffed her feet in the dirt. Peach pawed at them, playing as if Darby had paws, too.

"Knowing Aunty Cathy, she won't stay in bed half that long," Darby told the dog. "Unless . . ."

Shut up, Darby ordered herself.

Don't imagine a single thing that could go wrong. Megan only had one parent. That was unfair enough.

Peach barked and Darby looked up.

A plane popped out of a cloud and kept flying.

Above those clouds, hidden by blue sky, the stars

watched her fussing and fretting. If Jonah was right and stars were the eyes of heaven, they already knew what Monday would bring.

So there was no sense worrying about it.

"Everything will be fine," she told Peach. "And that's that."

Chapter 9

Darby followed Jonah into Sun House, where he stood sorting through some mail.

The kitchen smelled like Thanksgiving and it only took Darby one glance to see why.

True to her word, Aunty Cathy had taught the can of pumpkin the meaning of payback.

Two pies and four loaves of pumpkin bread sat on the kitchen counter.

Darby glanced at the kitchen clock. Both hands were straight up, but it was neither noon nor midnight.

Jonah looked up from the mail.

"The power's been coming and going all day," he said when he noticed her frown.

"And the phone?" Darby asked.

"Off and on."

Darby dialed her mother's cell phone number anyway. As she waited through clicking and a sound like someone rubbing a blanket on a microphone, Darby looked at the yellow sticky notes Aunty Cathy had used to label the loaves of pumpkin bread, one each for Kimo, Kit, Cade, and Tutu. She must have baked them before she agreed to go to the doctor.

A high-pitched beep made Darby hang up the phone. Suddenly she remembered Jonah had been riding away from the ranch when she'd left for school that morning.

"Was Tutu okay when you . . . ?" Darby's voice trailed off. Jonah stopped squinting at the mail to meet her eyes. He looked years older than he had yesterday. "Are you okay?"

"Why wouldn't I be?" Jonah asked. An irritated frown replaced the lines of exhaustion on his face. "Other than checking on your tutu—who laughed at all the excitement over the quake"—he put in with a wry smile—"I haven't done anything all day except pick up junk and drive that stubborn woman back and forth to town."

The day she arrived at the ranch, Kimo had told Darby that her grandfather didn't admire cowards. Given what she'd learned about Jonah since then, Darby guessed he'd probably think that admitting he was worried about the stock, ranch buildings, and

Cathy would make him seem weak.

So Darby tried a different approach to make sure he was all right.

"Just thought you might want a little nap," Darby said. Looking down, she kicked her boot toe at the floor Aunty Cathy had managed to scrub before going to the doctor. "We got going pretty early this morning."

Jonah's sudden roar of laughter startled Darby.

Her grandfather had seen through her no-big-deal mask to her concern but he obviously liked it better than her fussing over him.

"Darby Leilani Kealoha," he said with an appreciative chuckle, "you do have the stuff of a ranch girl."

If he'd given her a medal, Darby couldn't have been prouder.

Jonah's laughter subsided and he tapped his chest, saying, "This old man's not hurt, if that's what you're wanting to ask."

"Good," Darby said, lifting one shoulder in apology. "Because this morning, I was concentrating on the horses, instead of you—"

"That's exactly what you should have been doing," Jonah said. "I can take care of myself."

Darby stood even taller. But she knew she couldn't stick around, longing for a piece of pie when there was work to be done.

"What should I do first?" she asked her grandfather.

"Lead your filly up from the pasture. If she's going *holoholo*, she'd better learn to behave."

"Okay," Darby said slowly.

Don't bring it up, Darby told herself. Don't ask if he'll still let you go—and take Hoku!—if Megan has to stay behind with Aunty Cathy.

Could he have forgotten that Megan had been a condition of his approval?

"Tomorrow's soon enough for you to start walking along our fences, looking for loose posts or downed boards that mighta got wobbly after Cade rode through," Jonah said.

That would take a long time, but it shouldn't be hard, Darby thought.

"After you've brought Hoku home, go visit your tutu."

"Really?" Darby pushed loose tendrils of hair back toward her ponytail. She'd like to go interview her great-grandmother about Two Sisters, but even if Hoku was easy to catch, she wasn't sure she'd have time. "Can I get to Tutu's cottage and back before dark?"

"You won't have to ride that far," Jonah said.

"All right," Darby said, nodding. "Where should I meet her?"

"She'll find you," Jonah said with resignation, signifying what a burden it was having a mother known the island over as a wise woman or witch, depending on who you asked.

"Okay," Darby said, then started for the door.

"Granddaughter?" Jonah's voice caught Darby before she touched the doorknob. "You've got two days to show me you're not about to get bucked off again."

"I'll do it!" Darby promised, without thinking about how.

"And take your tutu this pumpkin bread when you go, yeah?" Jonah said.

"Yeah," Darby agreed, and then she was out the door.

Darby almost took the path down to the pastures on foot, but Hoku was used to being led beside Navigator—ponying, the cowboys called it—so Darby looked around for the coffee-colored gelding.

Darby was a little sorry she'd forgotten to replace her new fawn-colored boots for the scuffed ones she'd gotten as hand-me-downs from Megan, but not sorry enough to go back to the house and change.

She spotted Navigator, Biscuit, and Judge grazing over by the round pen. Their contented browsing made Darby's heart bump with joy. If she could have seen into the future from this time last year, she'd have been positive she was seeing a dream.

In that dream, she stood in nature's cupped hand, surrounded by impossibly green beauty as two bay horses—one big and strong, the other gray-muzzled and sweet—came to her.

But it was real, and Biscuit reminded her of that when he stayed put. Seeing his chance to eat alone, he began ripping at the grass as if he'd been starved.

Instead of coming to nuzzle her, Navigator trotted ahead of Darby, tossing his black mane, leading her toward the tack room.

"Good, 'Gator. You've forgotten all about yesterday, haven't you?"

The gelding's eagerness to be saddled and ridden convinced Darby she was right. Yesterday, Navigator had sensed the coming earthquake.

"And you've forgiven me for being so dense, right?"

Navigator didn't look back.

Judge tagged along behind Darby, lengthening his stride once to sniff at her pockets for treats.

"Sorry," Darby told the old horse, but Judge overcame his disappointment to neigh a greeting at Kit Ely.

The foreman stood on a ladder, tapping a metal pin into the top hinge on the tack-room door.

"If it's not the can-do *keiki*," Kit said before giving the pin one final tap.

Wow, Darby thought.

First Jonah's compliment, now Kit, a Nevada cowboy who must know what he was talking about, was calling her the "can-do kid."

It was a good thing no one could see inside her mind. If they could, they'd know she was wriggling like a proud puppy.

"Hi," she said.

Kit moved the door back and forth with experimental slowness.

"That's got 'er," he said, and climbed down. "Hoku's gear is laid out over her gate. I checked the fence for strain, where she was rammin' against it, and everything looks like it held."

Darby tried not to think about Hoku charging the fence with rolling eyes and determined terror that morning.

"Thank you," she said. "I'm going to pony her with Navigator."

"Well, now . . . ," Kit said, staring at Sun House as if he could see through its walls. "Jonah didn't talk to you about Navigator, then?"

"No!" Darby stared at the horse. "Was he hurt during the earthquake?"

"Nothin' like that," Kit said, and then he shook his head, whispering, "Ah, boss, why do you do me this way?"

Darby didn't like the sound of that.

"Huh?" she asked.

"All day, your grandpa's been touchy as a teased snake."

Of course, there were no snakes in Hawaii, Darby thought. But Kit was from Nevada. Darby's mind had set off on a detour when Kit crossed his arms. "So I'm not takin' him on about this."

"About what?" Darby asked.

Kit rubbed the back of his neck. He took off his black Stetson, brushed its brim, then put it back on.

"Judge'll be your saddle horse for the next couple of days," Kit said, squinting past her. "'Less you're under the boss's supervision."

"Judge," Darby repeated.

What could she say that wouldn't sound stuck-up, like she believed she was too good a rider for the older gelding, who'd sailed across the Pacific Ocean as Hoku's buddy?

"Okay," she said finally. But she didn't move. She had been riding for only a few weeks. She had no right to feel insulted. But how had she gone from the possibility of riding Hoku yesterday to Judge?

Sensing her bewilderment, Kit spoke up.

"I'll give him a quick brushing and tack him up. You get Hoku's gear," he said. Then, with a joking tone, Kit turned toward the horses. "C'mon, Judge, you old slacker. Your vacation's over."

Judge must have understood. His fuzzy ears pricked forward. He shouldered past Navigator and pressed his face into Kit's shirt, inhaling his scent as if the cowboy was all his.

Darby hurried to Hoku's empty corral. A flapping sound made Darby look up.

She stared into the branches of the ohia tree, looking for *pueo*, the round-faced owl. She could see a dangling branch that might have broken when the earth shook, but no bird.

Stop wasting time, she reminded herself.

Darby grabbed Hoku's halter and lead rope, gave a quick wave, just in case the Kealoha family's guardian animal was up there, offering its approval, then raced back to the tack shed.

A few minutes later, Kit shifted the cinched-on saddle, then considered it from in front of the horse to make sure it was centered. He tied Hoku's orange-and-white lead rope and halter on with saddle strings, then linked his hands together and nodded at them.

Darby would rather mount from a sidehill, but she took Kit's offer. Placing her left boot in his hands, she sprang into the saddle.

Judge gave an excited snort and tossed his head. As his mane flipped against his neck, Darby smelled the conditioner Kit had sprayed on Judge's mane, so he could brush out the tangles.

"Legs forward," he said, then adjusted the stirrups of the first saddle Judge had worn since he arrived in Hawaii.

Kit waved her off without advice, as if she were a seasoned rider. Darby liked that, but she was still feeling a little hurt that Jonah had moved her down to a gentler horse for something that wasn't her fault.

She glanced back over her shoulder at Navigator, who'd rejoined Biscuit. She reminded herself that she'd seen Kit, Cade, and Kimo, maybe Jonah, too, riding yesterday, and none of *them* had been thrown.

If Navigator had sensed the coming earthquake,

so had the other horses. Maybe Jonah had a point after all.

"That doesn't mean I have to like it," she complained to Judge.

But the Nevada gelding wouldn't let her dampen his mood. He arched his neck and neighed as they wound down the path to the lower pastures.

All of the other horses stopped grazing to stare at him, so Judge set his hooves in a flashy jog.

"You're allowed to show off," Darby told him. His gait was easy and smooth and Darby could picture him circling a herd of cattle, though he had simply arrived on this ranch and been put out to pasture.

As Darby leaned forward, Judge turned an ear to listen.

"I love you," Darby told the old gelding.

My heart's just up for grabs when it comes to horses, she thought.

With a smile on her face, Darby rode down to catch Hoku.

 Chapter 10

Hoku came along as if she remembered that Darby had made her promise to earlier that day. She was still a little spooky, spending at least ten minutes sniffing Judge, who must look different with a saddle and rider. The gate that Kit had left open got the same treatment, as if Hoku's senses had been sharpened by spending time with a community of horses.

Once she'd decided to enter her corral, Hoku gulped her hay and lowered herself to the ground, front legs tucked beneath her.

With Hoku content, Darby collected the loaf of pumpkin bread Aunty Cathy had made for Tutu from the kitchen, then rode Judge back through the pastures toward her great-grandmother's cottage.

Instead of being worn out by the ride, Judge took pleasure in exploring the Hawaii he'd only seen through fences.

Sunlight slanted through the rain-forest canopy, looking like golden strings on a huge Hawaiian harp. The trees were alive with birdsong, the gliding of leaves on leaves, and the burbling of an unseen stream.

Judge was equally mesmerized by the woods. His fuzzy ears pointed in different directions with each step. With wide nostrils, he sucked in unknown scents and savored them.

"You've never been past that fence, have you, boy?" Darby asked, petting Judge's coarse black mane. "Anything could happen here."

"He's a long way from Nevada." Tutu's voice floated to Darby, but she couldn't see her great-grandmother yet.

Judge didn't shy. He must have sensed the old woman and her horse on their way.

"Aloha!" Tutu called.

Once more, Darby thought her great-grand-mother's voice belonged to a jolly lady of larger proportions, instead of an old woman who was as slender as a girl.

"Aloha," Darby called back.

Bare of saddle and bridle, Prettypaint entered the clearing. The blue-gray mare was old, but lovely. Her head nodded to the left side of the path, then the right, greeting throngs of invisible admirers. Silken feathers drifted above hooves placed with exquisite care, as if she bore a treasure on her back.

Tutu rode in a billowing pink skirt. Her white hair streamed over her right shoulder. An owl rode on her left.

"Yes, Prettypaint, this is Judge. He came across the ocean with Hoku." Tutu addressed the mare as if she were human, and Darby longed for her mother to see how Tutu had pampered the horse she'd left behind.

Darby wanted to rush up and stroke the dusky nose the horse extended her way. She didn't, partly because Jonah's warnings were ringing in her mind, but mostly because she took her cue from Judge. The gelding hung back, head lowered in respect.

"We were coming to see you," Darby said.

"This way?" Tutu asked. "Keep going along this trail and you'll end up at the old sugar plantation."

"Really?" Darby asked.

"Really," Tutu insisted. "I wouldn't encourage you to explore the plantation. At least, not alone."

Darby twisted in her saddle. The red-dirt path behind her looked so familiar, but just as she'd told Judge, anything could happen in this forest.

She looked back as Tutu lifted the hand that had held a lock of pearl-colored mane. She gave a light clap. Hearing it, Prettypaint curled one foreleg up, slid the other foreleg ahead of her, and bowed, so that

Tutu could slip off her back.

"She's so graceful," Darby said, then remembered what she'd carried from the ranch kitchen. "I brought you some pumpkin bread."

She leaned down to hand Tutu the aluminum-foil-wrapped loaf before dismounting, then told her great-grandmother that Aunty Cathy had made it and explained what she knew of her concussion.

"I'm glad she saw a doctor," Tutu said, "but she'll be fine. That girl wouldn't have lasted this long at 'Iolani Ranch if she didn't have a hard head."

Darby laughed, and when Tutu suggested they share some pumpkin bread while they talked, she sat next to her great-grandmother on a log.

Preoccupied with keeping hold of Judge's reins, she'd forgotten all about the owl.

Drawing up on the tips of his claws as if he were about to take flight, the owl swept both wings toward Darby.

"Other side?" Tutu suggested apologetically. She patted a place for Darby to sit on her right, then tsked her tongue. "What a selfish bird you are."

Darby moved. She wanted no squabble with this owl she'd once seen munching on the head of a mouse.

After it flashed her a yellow-eyed glare, the owl preened, as if Darby had ruffled its feathers.

"Jonah tells me you're making a pilgrimage up Two Sisters," Tutu said.

Pilgrimage struck Darby as an oddly spiritual word, but she didn't want to correct Tutu, so she just said, "It's for an Ecology class project."

"Of course," Tutu said. "But you'll want to respect the Fire Maiden."

"Pele?" Darby asked. She'd seen pictures of the long-limbed goddess with a cloud of smoke-black hair. "I've never heard her called the Fire Maiden."

"Few have heard of her life on Wild Horse Island," Tutu said with a nod.

Darby gave a little bounce of excitement. "That's exactly what I was hoping we could talk about. My teacher Mr. Silva wants us to see how story connects with science."

"He sounds like a wise man," Tutu said.

Darby nodded, but her brain picked that moment to replay Tyson's warning. *Shouldn't go mocking Pele . . . she's one bad lady when she's mad.*

"Do people believe in her? Like she's real?" Darby blurted.

"Many believe. Some think she's a ghost of a once-live woman and others think she's always been a goddess. Most see her as a safety net."

"A safety net?" Darby asked.

"They have their daily faith, much like other modern people, but they leave offerings for Pele, and don't violate the *kapus* she's set."

"Like what?" Darby asked, as a surge of enthusiasm replaced Tyson's creepy voice.

"Don't pick the red lehua flowers from her beloved ohia trees without proper respect, and never swallow 'ohelo berries without offering them to her first. Pele is demanding and jealous, but she's spent thousands of years being thwarted by her big sister."

A tiny snort interrupted Tutu. Lulled by the sound of the old woman's voice, the owl had fallen asleep.

Tutu and Darby looked at each other and smiled.

"If you stay in the islands, you'll hear a hundred Pele stories, but the ones that feel truest to me are those I grew up with, here on Wild Horse Island."

"Perfect," Darby said.

"In her early days, Pele was simply looking for a home she could share with her big, brawling family. Of them all, only Pele was protective of the youngest sibling, a baby sister called Hi'iaka. Pele took her everywhere—"

"Is she the one . . ." Darby interrupted, then hesitated.

She'd never heard this story before, and yet a sparkle of memory told her that Pele always carried—meaning no disrespect to the goddess—a pet egg.

"Pele's little sister was in an egg. To keep her warm, Pele carried Hi'iaka in her armpit," Tutu filled in good-naturedly.

But how did I know that? Darby wondered.

The next part of the legend sounded familiar, too.

Pele dug warm earth-sheltered homes for her family, but her oldest sister, the sea goddess, hated feeling cozy. She lived in cold seawater but still longed to be with her family. So, because she was the stronger of the two goddesses, the sea goddess made sure water bubbled up from beneath Pele's creations, or crashed over them in the form of huge waves. And even when Pele moved to the next island, and the next, her sister followed.

"Sometimes Pele got mad and fought back. She threw hot rocks to scare her sister. Boulders with fiery comet tails flew through the air, and rivers of fire followed. But the sea goddess caught the manifestations of Pele's rage with her cold watery hands, molded them a bit, and patted them onto the edges of the islands, making more land.

"It was only when Pele reached the big island of Hawaii that the sisters worked out a truce. The sea goddess allowed Pele and her family to live in the volcano of Kilauea, in a warm lava lake."

"So she's not here?" Darby asked hesitantly.

"Sometimes she is," Tutu said, smiling. "When our little island appeared in the shadow of Hawaii, Pele saw it as the perfect place for her little sister. Hi'iaka's Playpen is the old name for Wild Horse Island.

"It was a peaceful place, where the sisters and brothers took turns babysitting. Sometimes Pele would be here, and you can see her favorite plants to prove it. Sometimes brother Moho, the god of steam, was here in the form of a powerful white stallion."

"Wow," Darby said. Now the story was heading in a direction she liked. "And that's why the name changed to Wild Horse Island?"

"For him, and for another brother, the god of thunderclouds, who amused Hi'iaka by taking the form of a black stallion to race with Moho. Sometimes Pele joined her brothers' races, taking the form of a wild filly whose coat was the color of the flames that danced across the surface of Kilauea's lava lake, and then she was called the Fire Maiden."

Darby sighed and hugged her arms around herself, feeling goose bumps. Finally, sounding a little sappy, she said, "And then everyone lived happily ever after."

"Usually," Tutu said. "But the sea goddess is not very good about taking her turn at babysitting, and sometimes Pele must storm around our island, stomping her feet and stirring the warmth inside our volcanoes, to summon her sister. And when the sea goddess at last shows up, she plays a little too rough, creating storms and tsunamis."

For an instant Darby thought of a big, strong girl like Duckie showing off to amuse a baby, but then she thought of her assignment. Pele's stomping could be earthquakes. When she stoked up the fiery warmth her sister hated, that could be the bubbling lava and eruptions. And then the tsunamis. It would be easy enough to braid science and story together, but Darby felt a little worried.

"That's how it really happens, too, isn't it?" she asked. "Earthquakes, then eruptions and tsunamis."

"Sometimes. But don't worry, Darby Leilani. After all, Pele chose this as her little sister's playpen." Tutu's arm pulled Darby against her in a hug, but suddenly the tropical world around them didn't seem so safe.

"It's just that I don't know all her rules and regulations," Darby said, and she realized she was holding Judge's reins so tightly, she'd scratched the leather with her fingernails.

"There's only one rule to remember," Tutu said. "When I was a little girl, there was a rhyme about it. Let me see . . ."

Darby didn't mean to be holding her breath, but as she waited, she was.

"I think I have it," Tutu said. She still held Darby against her shoulder, and she tilted her head against Darby's as she recited. "Red is her color, black is her hair. Respect Fire Maiden, or I warn you: beware."

Chapter 11

Daylight lasted until Darby sighted the broodmare pasture and then, as if someone had pulled a silver curtain, fog crept over 'Iolani Ranch, blurring the edges of the foreman's house and Sun House.

She took her time grooming Judge, checking his feet for stones and feeling his legs for hot spots, since this was his longest journey carrying a rider for some time. Actually, the old horse seemed revitalized by the ride and reluctant to move off and eat, even when Darby released him.

When she walked into Sun House's kitchen, Darby didn't mention the missing pie, but she noticed. Her guess was that it had been carried upstairs to Aunty Cathy.

Without Cathy Kato in charge, the ranch wouldn't run smoothly for long. She not only cooked and kept the ranch finances straight, she monitored the interaction between domestic animals and Hawaiian wildlife. And even though he wouldn't admit it, Jonah knew Aunty Cathy's background in tourism could help save the ranch if tougher times came.

Even now, as they picked through the newly organized cupboards for a semblance of dinner, Darby could see Jonah trying to listen through the ceiling. She'd bet her grandfather had used delivery of the pie as an excuse to go up and see how Aunty Cathy and Megan were doing.

Darby wanted a slab of that pie for her own, too, but first she sat down with a sandwich and milk.

When Jonah balanced a mound of unheated pork-fried rice on a plate and headed for the lanai, Darby asked if she could just sit at the kitchen table and call Ann.

"Have at it," Jonah said with an offhand gesture.

Darby learned that the same sort of casual evening was going on at Ann's house. Together they ate, talked about Aunty Cathy's concussion and Darby's interview with Tutu, and in whispers, the possibility that Megan would not be able to ride along on their research trip. Finally, Darby told Ann that she'd been grounded from Navigator.

"Do you fall off a lot?" Ann asked.

"Well, no, but I'm not off to a good start. Really,"

Darby said when she heard Ann giggle, "I've come close a bunch of times. Like, dozens."

"I think I know your problem," Ann said.

Darby waited in silence.

"Let's see," Ann said. "You've been riding for, what? A couple months? And you never rode before, did you?"

"Well, no, but—"

"Not around in a ring, not up and down a bridle path, or anything, and now, suddenly, you're in situations that even a real paniolo would find challenging. The whole thing with wild pigs, idiots like Manny." Ann lowered her voice. "Oh, and let's not forget earthquakes!"

"If I put it that way to my mom," Darby said quietly, "she'd probably think it was child abuse."

"Not if she rode as a kid," Ann declared. "She did, right?"

"That's what they tell me."

"She'd probably understand, then. I mean, I've been riding all my life. Really, my mom has a photo of my dad carrying me around on his cutting horse when I was just a month old. And sometimes I still fall, or slip off to keep from being bucked off. I hate it worse than poison, but it happens if you push yourself." Ann paused, and Darby heard a voice in the background.

"My mom says I have to get off," Ann said, "but she also says she's looking forward to meeting you when we pick up you and the horses on Monday."

"Tell her I'm looking forward to meeting her and your dad, too," Darby said politely, then added, "I'll remember everything Tutu said and be the storyteller while we're riding."

"This is going to be so much fun," Ann said.

"I can hardly wait," Darby agreed.

Just as Darby hung up, footsteps sounded on the Katos' stairs. Jonah already had the front door open.

"Do you need my help?" he asked.

"No," Megan said, looking surprised at his greeting. "My mom says that since she has to stay awake, she might as well be lazy and watch whatever's on television."

"Good," Jonah said. "That's what I told her to do, and she needs something to eat. Soup, maybe. She wanted to stop for groceries, but the market was too busy. People restocking ruined food," he explained, and Darby could imagine Aunty Cathy wanting to stop for food and Jonah insisting on bringing her home, per the doctor's orders.

"She just wants a soda and popcorn." Megan barely got the words out before Jonah stalked toward the cupboards and flung open door after door. "I can fix it," she added.

"I'll do it," Jonah said.

He sounded so determined, Megan just shrugged and rolled her eyes at Darby. When their eyes met, Darby was pretty sure Megan had figured out what she just had: Jonah was in the habit of being the boss. When an accident happened, maybe he couldn't be in control. But he could be in charge. Even if that only meant making popcorn.

A few minutes later, Jonah had drizzled the popcorn with melted butter and handed it to Megan. She was just about to leave when she stopped and pointed at Darby. "My mom wanted me to make sure you'd called Ellen back."

"My mom called?" Darby asked.

"Yeah. Of course, she might have been a little confused," Megan said, "but she told me that she left something"—Megan turned and scanned the refrigerator—"here." She tapped a note in Aunty Cathy's handwriting.

"How could I have missed that?" Darby wondered out loud.

Megan was gone by the time Darby turned toward Jonah. He'd seen her trying to call her mother at least twice. Why hadn't he mentioned that her mother had gotten through?

"Don't worry," he said, nodding toward the yellow note. "Cathy musta told her no one was killed by that little quake."

"Not so little," Darby said. "Six point oh."

Jonah shrugged.

Darby didn't like confrontations with anyone, and she and Jonah were just moving past the one from last night, but the flutter in her stomach wasn't a good enough reason to back down.

Hands on her hips, Darby said, "Plus, that was hours ago. I've been thinking my mom was so worried!"

She was prepared for Jonah to come back at her with a roar. For a minute, his gaze locked on hers, but then he closed his eyes and pinched the bridge of his nose. When he opened his eyes again, he just looked tired.

"Truly, Granddaughter, I forgot," Jonah confessed. "I am sorry."

Unsettled by his apology, Darby said, "Uh, that's okay. I'll try to call her again now."

But the phone rang just as Darby reached for it. "Hello?"

"What did you break?" Ellen demanded.

"Nothing, Mom."

"I mean, body parts, not fine china," she urged.

"Mom, I'm fine. I didn't even get a bruise. Honest!"

She heard her mother's sigh before she went on a bit more calmly, "But with the intensity of that earthquake, Darby, there had to be damage everywhere. What about your horse?"

Darby felt a glow like candlelight in her chest. Ellen knew what was most important to her daughter.

"Hoku is just great," Darby began, and then she described how they'd set all the horses free, and her mom sounded excited. When she explained how the

impromptu herd had assembled to protect themselves, her mother said she wished television cameras
had been there to catch it. And when Darby admitted
wearing her short pink nightgown to tromp down to
the pasture, her mother laughed and said she'd bet
that had been something to see.

With a pleased sigh, Ellen asked, "And you went
to school?"

Did it take distance to make you really appreciate
your mother? Darby wondered. Twice, Ellen had
zeroed in on what Darby held important: first horses,
then school.

She explained about the delayed start, and had
started detailing her science and story project before
she bit her tongue, afraid her mother wouldn't
approve of her riding up to Two Sisters.

It was like Ellen read her mind.

"Don't even think of going alone," she said.

"I won't. I'm going with two other girls. Megan's
older and she's been raised on the ranch."

"Okay," Ellen said cautiously. "Just the same,
don't go past the stone trees."

"What are the stone trees?" Darby asked.

"Only one of the best things on the island." Her
mother sounded as if she was bragging about her
birthplace, and Darby was pretty sure she'd never
heard her do that before. "Sometime thousands of
years ago, lava covered the trees, but the trunks and
branches inside lasted long enough that they gave

form to the lava before it hardened. Of course, there's a less scientific explanation, too."

Maybe it was the long, tiring day that made tears spring to Darby's eyes when her mother's voice turned dreamy. But Darby didn't let on that she was touched by her mother's tone. If Ellen thought she was crying, or hiding something, she'd have her on the next plane back home.

Darby cleared her throat and asked, "Is there a story to them? Would Tutu be able to tell me?"

"Of course she would," Ellen said. "You know, she's my grandmother and she did her best to help me through a very difficult time. But she seems like something out of a fairy tale now."

"She's still here, and she's real," Darby said. "I just saw her today for my project."

"Next time, tell her I miss her, will you?" Ellen said, and then she cleared her throat before adding, "So that's what you have planned for spring break? Homework?"

"Pretty much," Darby said.

"Well, have a little fun, too."

Darby thought her mother was about to hang up, but she seemed unwilling to end their talk.

"When I talked with Cathy—who was very understanding, but a little preoccupied—"

"The whole kitchen kind of caved in," Darby explained. "It looked like a gigantic tossed salad, except there were pots and pans mixed in."

"I know she mentioned something breaking," Ellen insisted. "That's why I was worried about your arms and legs."

"Well." Darby looked around at the neat kitchen, then gazed out the window. "It could have been almost anything. The foundation on the foreman's house cracked, and a horse got locked inside the tack room and tried to paw his way out, plus lots of glassware broke. . . ."

"But you're all fine?"

"All except Aunty Cathy. She got hit on the head with, uh, I think she said a number ten can of pumpkin."

"My goodness, is she all right?"

"She saw the doctor—"

"Will wonders never cease," Ellen interjected, but Darby wasn't sure what she meant by that, so she went on.

"And she has a concussion, so she's upstairs resting."

The silence that hummed over the line lasted so long, Darby was pretty sure that she and her mother had been cut off.

"Mom?"

"That's a shame about the concussion, but Darby, did you say 'upstairs'?" Ellen asked.

Now it was Darby's turn to be quiet while she thought. Aunty Cathy had told Darby during the first week she was here that Jonah had built the little upstairs apartment for Ellen, hoping she'd come home if she could have her own private space. But she hadn't come home.

"You know, Mom," Darby nudged her mother's memory, "the little apartment over Sun House that Jonah built for you? But I guess you never saw it, so maybe you forgot it was there."

"Maybe I forgot a lot of things about Jonah." Her mom's wistful tone had turned unforgiving, but she got her voice back under control so quickly, Darby wondered if she'd imagined the change. "I'm glad you're having fun and doing things you won't be able to do at home, honey."

"Like riding on the slope of our family volcanoes?" Darby suggested.

"Exactly," Ellen said. "Because a trip to Wild Horse Island only comes once in a lifetime."

Chapter 12

Aftershock!

Darby's bed swayed. Instantly awake, she ordered her feet to run outside. Then Darby realized she wasn't alone.

"Darby . . . " Jonah stood so close to her bed, she smelled leather polish on his boots. He was shaking her shoulder.

"What? Was there an aftershock?"

"Probably hundreds of 'em, but not just now. The telephone. It's for you. I came in because I didn't want to yell and wake them upstairs," he explained.

Darby blinked her bedroom into focus. Sunlight streamed through her window, spotlighting her lucky bamboo plant, so it wasn't early.

The telephone. It could only be Ann or her mom, or maybe her dad had finally gotten through to check on her.

Darby didn't glance at the clock. She'd stayed up way too late last night. She'd written in her journal, stared at her bedroom ceiling, and listened to the Katos' television, which she could hear quite clearly if she laid still.

Her mind had darted from Judge's ability to climb the slopes of Two Sisters, to wondering what her mother had meant when she'd said a trip to Wild Horse Island was a once-in-a-lifetime experience. And when she finally did fall asleep, she dreamed she was clinging to the mane of a fog-white stallion, racing against a black mustang with one blue eye. And coming up behind them all, she'd seen Hoku. Except it wasn't Hoku, it was Fire Maiden, the horse incarnation of Pele. . . .

"Shall I tell him to call back?" Jonah asked.

Darby had been about to doze off again, but Jonah's voice snapped her awake.

Shall I tell *him* to call back, that's what Jonah had asked, right? Him, so it must be Dad.

"No. I'm up. Honest," Darby assured her grandfather.

Barefoot, she followed Jonah down the hall, toward the kitchen aromas of coffee and toast, and grabbed up the phone.

"Hello?" Darby said, but she only heard a click,

then a dial tone. Jonah looked at her with raised eye-brows.

"Whoever it was hung up," she said, answering his silent question. "Got tired of waiting, I guess."

"Some phone and power lines are still down from the earthquake," Jonah suggested, but just then the phone rang once more.

"I'll get it," Darby said. "Hello?"

The caller clicked off. Again.

"Someone's pranking you," Jonah said. "A boy about your age, by his voice."

Tyson, Darby thought immediately. But why?

"You know who it is," Jonah said.

"No, I—well, maybe," Darby admitted.

"The Tyson kid that Kimo told me about?"

Too tired to argue about the latest invasion of her privacy, Darby sagged forward until her chin rested on her crossed arms on the kitchen tabletop.

"And they say girls gossip too much," she grumbled.

"The ranch, it's like a *kipuka*, yeah?" Jonah said unapologetically.

Darby knew about *kipukas*.

To be alone with Hoku, she'd crossed a bed of spiky *a'a'* lava, until she'd reached an island of rainforested oasis. With rainwater pools and wildlife, it was a world with beauties and problems all its own.

She supposed Jonah, in his storyteller's way, was trying to excuse his prying.

"So, this Ty character called you a haole crab, yeah?" Jonah asked.

"Yeah, but Ann said he might not have meant anything bad by it."

"Why make excuses for him? If he didn't mean to hurt your feelings, he would've stayed on the phone just now. And he wouldn't have called you haole crab, but *malihini*."

"That's like a newcomer, right?" Darby asked. She still felt awkward using Hawaiian words, but she was picking up a lot of them.

This time, she was right. She could tell by Jonah's pleased nod.

"You know, I didn't do anything to Tyson or his friend."

"You didn't have to." Jonah must have seen that his response didn't satisfy her, because he went on. "He did it because he could. Guy don't feel so good about himself? He wants everybody down in the dumps."

"I guess," Darby said.

"I'm not one to give advice"—Darby almost laughed—"about personal stuff, but this Tyson mentioning crabs reminds me of something your tutu told me when I was your age.

"I didn't get on well at school. My father was what educated people called an eccentric. Most just wrote him off as an oddball. So, no matter what I tried to do at school, I was that oddball's kid.

"Then your tutu told me school is like a bucket of crabs, all trying to get on top."

A bucket of crabs. Darby pictured dozens of pointed, pinkish legs thrashing and clacking together.

"Sometimes they climb over. Just as often, they get pushed under. And maybe their claws clamp onto another crab and drag him down, too."

It didn't take Darby long to make sense of the story. Her cousin Duckie had made it onto the team and clawed her way to the top, beating out athletes from other schools and other leagues. When she'd learned Darby was a good swimmer, too, Duckie did everything she could to remain number one on the school's swim team, even getting Darby in trouble with the swim coach.

Honors students were no different than athletes. Darby knew from experience that getting an A wasn't enough. The minute graded work was returned, the kids checked out each other's papers, hoping their A was worth more points than anyone else's.

When Darby's mind circled back to Ty, she supposed he was the same. It just made sense that all the tough kids wanted to be the toughest.

Ty must have gotten some bad information somewhere, Darby thought, *if he believes he'll look tougher by dragging me down.*

Suddenly Jonah set a mug of hot chocolate on the table, next to Darby's hand, and she realized he'd been making it while she stared off into space.

"What did Tutu tell you to do about, you know, all the other crabs?" she asked Jonah.

"She didn't. I decided on my own that there was no place for me in that bucket."

"You didn't drop out of school!" Darby stared up at Jonah, who still stood next to her. His grin seemed to be applause for her appalled tone.

"No, I just got outta the way and let 'em pinch each other." Jonah turned toward the kitchen window. "After a while, just dodgin' their claws wasn't enough for me. I tipped the bucket over and crawled away home."

Hands on hips, Jonah faced her, picked up his cup of coffee, and took a sip before saying, "Turns out this is the only place in the world I cared about being on top."

Darby took a deep breath and released it.

What if I feel exactly the same way? she thought.

Darby didn't have time to ponder the idea before Jonah demanded, "Haven't I told you not to let me waste time talkin' story?"

"No, but—"

"It's time I checked on the invalid." Jonah pointed up toward the Katos' apartment.

But Jonah didn't go anywhere; he just asked, "How'd you like Judge?"

"Judge is great," Darby said. "I'm not sure he's in shape for climbing, though."

Jonah waited.

"So, if I'm going to ride up to Two Sisters to do this school project . . ." Darby let the sentence dangle, but Jonah didn't take the bait.

"Better get some breakfast down, before you start your chores," he said.

Darby realized she was going to have to come right out and ask him if he'd allow her to ride Navigator on her trip.

"When I got home from school on Thursday, you seemed to agree with Kit that Hoku was ready to start carrying a rider—" she began, and this time Jonah cut her off.

"I still think she is," he said, looking puzzled.

"Oh." Darby's sigh left her feeling both deflated and excited at the same time. "I thought because of what happened with Navigator—"

"What's that got to do with Hoku?" Jonah's head was tilted to one side. "She's ready to be saddle-schooled. I'm just not sure that you should be her first rider."

Darby wouldn't have believed her heartbeats could drown out Jonah's words, but that's exactly what was happening.

"Megan's the right size. Or your friend, crazy Ann . . ."

"You changed your mind because of the earth-quake?" Darby asked faintly.

"I haven't changed my mind. I'm still deciding. And it has nothing to do with the earthquake."

"It does," Darby insisted. "Research says animals can be early-warning systems for earthquakes. I'll find you articles to prove it. And"—Darby took a breath, searching her mind for more evidence—"remember how the dogs were howling? And when Francie broke loose? She never does that! And Joker was pawing at the bunkhouse door, all sweating and nervous the night before."

"So, you think Navigator's bucking was all about what was under his feet, and had nothing to do with who was on his back?" Jonah demanded.

"Yes! No. Well, mostly it didn't," Darby nearly shouted.

"*Shh.*" Jonah made a lowering motion with his hand. "That mean you want another chance?"

"Of course I—"

"Because I'm telling you, Granddaughter," Jonah warned, "once you girls get up on Two Sisters, you're on your own for a while. No cell phone works up there. The university's monitoring station is outdated and unstaffed. It's a steep ride up and a roller coaster comin' back down."

Was Jonah talking himself out of letting her go?

"The only shortcut down is one you don't want to take with that filly of yours," he said.

"I'm not sure Judge can make that climb. I

wouldn't force him if he wasn't in shape for it," Darby said, and Jonah could tell that she wasn't just making an excuse.

"I know," Jonah said.

"That's the main reason I'd like another chance to prove I can ride Navigator. I know he'll take me all the way to the top and back down."

Jonah rubbed his right ring finger, the one a long-ago teacher had broken with a ruler because he'd spoken Hawaiian in class.

"You got yourself a bargain, Granddaughter. Show me you can ride three horses safely"—Darby pictured herself standing with a foot on the backs of each of two horses while another ran in between— "and we'll see about Navigator. And as soon as you get home, we'll go back to saddle-schooling Hoku."

"Thank you." Darby's eyes closed in gratitude.

Darby hurried to her room to change into jeans, but first she sat on her bed and took a deep breath. She did it again and still couldn't hear herself wheezing.

She hadn't had asthma for days, but her chest felt tight. Taking her inhaler on the camping trip would be good insurance, and it should only take her a minute to find it.

She was looking through her dresser drawers when voices from overhead sifted down to her.

"Jonah, there's smoke on the mountain. Don't tell me you're letting her go?"

"It's mist."

Even though she couldn't see Jonah talking to Aunty Cathy, she knew that tone of his. Her grandfather's eyes would look black. He'd stand solid as a wall, certain that he was right.

"This isn't a good idea." Aunty Cathy sounded just as sure that *she* was right.

On her first day at 'Iolani Ranch, Darby had realized Aunty Cathy had a different relationship with Jonah than anyone else. He didn't intimidate her, so she spoke her mind.

Now, they lowered their voices. Quick sentences flew back and forth, but Darby couldn't decode them through the ceiling.

Not until Jonah's words rang as clearly as if he'd shouted into a microphone.

"I don't know how long she'll be here. Or if she'll ever come back. Riding up her own volcano." Jonah's awe painted a picture that made Darby shiver. "Think of that, and tell me for certain she'll ever do anything like that, ever again?"

". . . dangerous . . ."

"Hawaiian volcanoes are slow and quiet, remember?" For a moment, Jonah sounded as if he was teasing, but then his voice turned sad. "Cathy, when she's an old woman, she'll remember the Two Sisters and maybe, if she's lucky, Pele's fireworks, too. I can give that to Darby. Why shouldn't I?"

Aunty Cathy was insisting something when

Jonah boomed, ". . . Ellen too close. Never let her go anywhere or do anything, just in case."

Light footsteps went up the stairway to the Katos' apartment. The door opened and then Darby heard Megan's voice.

No wonder Aunty Cathy and Jonah had been having such an unusual conversation. They had—or at least they thought they'd had—no audience.

Darby walked to the entrance hall, sat on the bench, pulled on her boots, and sighed.

It was totally frustrating that she couldn't ask for clarification about what she'd heard, because she'd learned it all by snooping.

Chapter 13

Darby's lessons in controlling excited mounts began with a ride on Lady Wong.

The mare wasn't her choice. Her involvement was limited to answering one question.

"Which horses have you ridden on this ranch?" Jonah asked.

"Kona, Luna, Navigator, and Judge," Darby said.

After that, four cowboys—Cade, Jonah, Kimo, and Kit—made all the decisions for her, until she mounted up.

"No mares," Kit pointed out.

"What if I try her on Tango?" Jonah asked the foreman.

Kit caught his breath. Cade gave a violent shake of his head.

"Okay, not Tango, but the horse has to be a challenge," Jonah said.

"Lady Wong," Kimo suggested. "She's all lead mare these days, and there's her colt. . . ."

"Not Biscuit," Kit mused, then turned to Cade and asked, "How about your horse?"

"Joker will buck going into a lope sometimes. . . ." Cade nodded slowly as if that was a good thing.

"So she'd know what to anticipate, when to be ready," Kimo said.

"What about that palomino, Doubloon?" Kit asked. "Think he's too green?"

"Too fast," Jonah said.

"Not even as a final exam?" Cade asked. He and Kit glanced at Darby, as if they could already picture her astride the palomino, but Jonah was shaking his head.

"I don't want him frustrated by the round pen. I've got plans for that boy," Jonah admitted.

"Could use Baxter," Kimo said.

"Buckin' Baxter?" Darby interrupted.

Since no one even glanced at her, Darby decided that was a good place to stop talking.

Passing this test meant she could ride Navigator, not Judge. And she hoped to pick up tricks that would help her ride Hoku when the time came.

She wasn't really scared, just worried she'd end

up under Baxter's hooves if the fractious blue roan actually swapped ends, as she'd seen him do with Kimo.

"Horse doesn't have a mean bone in his body," Kimo assured her.

"It's not *his* bones I'm worried about," Darby muttered, but no one was listening, except maybe Cade.

Grinning, the young paniolo said, "Aw, Baxter just likes to have a little fun."

So Darby's final lineup of mounts was: Lady Wong, Joker, and Buckin' Baxter.

She'd ride the first two right away, Jonah told her.

"And you can have nightmares about Baxter tonight," Kimo teased her as he brought Lady Wong, with her colt Black Cat, up to the round pen.

"This is one mannerly mare," Jonah said, standing at the gray's head, while Kimo held her colt outside the round pen. "She was raced before I got her and never gave any trouble in the starting gates or elsewhere. But she'll want to stop each time she gets near her colt."

In the saddle now, Darby noticed how much leaner the mare felt than Judge or Navigator.

Black Cat whinnied plaintively. Even though milk still clung to his whiskers, he pretended he was starving. And abandoned.

Lady Wong breathed faster. Her front hooves

shifted. Finally, she tossed her head toward Jonah, but she became totally still when he moved to hold both cheek straps of her bridle. He stood in front of her, unmoving, until her head dipped.

"Wasn't she asking you to let her go?" Darby asked. Even though Jonah hadn't said or done anything harsh, taking her space and making her drop her head was discipline.

"Not exactly," Jonah said. "She told me I was just another horse. Next thing, if I let her get by with that, her ears would go back and she'd be sizing me up for a bite."

Darby drew a shaky breath. She had so much left to learn about horses.

"All you need to do is keep her going forward," Jonah said, checking the gray's cinch. "This mare's a leader, so you've gotta earn her respect. Don't let it cross her mind that she's bigger and stronger than you are."

"Okay," Darby said, lifting her reins until she felt the mare's mouth.

"If we were training her, we'd do it without distractions," Jonah explained, "like you did with Hoku in the *kipuka*. But we're training *you* to ride through those distractions, because sometimes they're gonna happen. Go."

Even though Darby gave Lady Wong the slightest of kicks, the mare bolted forward as if stung by a bee.

"Relax," Jonah said. "Keep your seat in the saddle."

Everything went fine until they neared Black Cat. Lady Wong wanted to stop, and Jonah's instructions came down like a hailstorm.

"Use your calves to drive her on. . . . Let's trot. . . . Your hands are bouncing . . . put them down . . . in front of her withers, one on each side. . . . You won't fall. . . . Look up, not down. . . ."

Darby's head was spinning by the time Jonah told her to stop Lady Wong, back her, make her stand quietly for a full two minutes, then dismount.

Next came Joker.

"It's not his fault," Cade said as he adjusted his stirrups to fit Darby's shorter legs. "When I first rode him, he'd buck when he went into a lope, and I let him." Cade glanced at Jonah and shrugged. "I know, it's a good way to wreck a horse, but I was just a kid. I thought it was cool to ride a bucking Appaloosa. And when Manny saw him acting up that way, he didn't think he could sell him, so he gave him to me.

"After that, I encouraged Joker to buck whenever Manny was watching."

"How long did it take him to figure out what you were doing?" Jonah asked.

"Six months," Cade said. "Then he let me have it good."

Nausea twisted Darby's stomach and she said, "Bad."

"What?" Cade asked.

"He let you have it bad. There's nothing good

about that little bully hitting you."

For a minute, Darby thought Cade would walk away.

Maybe this wasn't any of her business, but she'd met Manny and seen the way he swung his rifle around while taunting Cade.

"All I know is, after he was done with me, Manny said he'd sell Joker to someone who would treat him just the same. And I started planning my getaway."

Jonah nodded at Cade, approving the decision as he glanced at Darby and said, "Tipped over the bucket of crabs."

"What?" Cade asked.

"Big time," Darby replied, nodding.

If Cade could stop Manny from keeping him around as a convenient victim, she could stand up for who she was, to people like Tyson or Duckie.

The next time Tyson sneered at her at school or made one of his creepy phone calls, she'd remember Cade.

Looking between her and Jonah, Cade pulled his hala hat down firmly, gave up on understanding them, and led Joker over for her to mount.

"You're going to ride him from a walk, to a jog, then a lope," Jonah said.

As Darby swung into the saddle, the feisty Appaloosa swung his head around. He gave an accusing snort.

"And I should expect him to buck before the

lope?" Darby asked.

"Let's just see," Jonah told her.

Darby squeezed her legs. Joker gave a slashing swish of his black tail, but he didn't step out.

"Cluck him up," Jonah said.

Darby clucked, closed her boot heels against him in a little kick, and Joker obeyed, but he moved with the same stiff reluctance Navigator had shown the other day.

Something was wrong. She could feel it and so could the little Appaloosa. He moved into a trot on his own, and though Darby saw Jonah shake his head, she didn't pull Joker back down to a walk. She was waiting for—

"Whoa!" Kimo shouted from across the ranch yard.

He wasn't talking to a horse, but to the earth.

"You're okay, boy," Darby said, trying to urge Joker forward as he shied sideways.

"Did you feel that?" Megan called from the top of the stairs.

"Good boy, Joker. You didn't buck, and it was so scary. You felt it coming, didn't you?"

"Just an aftershock," Jonah shouted to Megan.

"Easy for you to say!" Megan called back, then slammed the door.

"Sassy kid," Jonah grumbled, then sized up Darby and Joker. "How'd you teach him to side pass?"

"Not funny," Darby said, but she smiled and kept

Joker turning in the direction in which he was heading. When she finally had him aimed in the direction
where they'd started out, she put him into a jog.

Joker snorted at Cade each time they passed him
on the fence.

The guy looked awful, Darby thought. Like an
anxious father, his frown was fixed on Joker, and he
tugged at his collar until his shirt hung at a weird
angle. He held his hat in one hand, while the other
pushed nonexistent hair out of his face over and over
again.

Brother, Cade had called this horse, and he must be
afraid she'd hurt him.

When Jonah told her to move Joker into a lope,
Darby gave it a try.

The Appaloosa jumped forward. Darby pulled
back on the reins. Then Jonah walked toward them,
and Joker ran in place for a few seconds before stopping.

"Okay, this is what happened," Jonah said, as if
he were dissecting a crime. "He was too spirited for
whoever rode him before Cade. They kicked him into
a lope and when he went, they yanked back on his
mouth. Every time, they had to kick him harder
because he knew they were going to hurt him when
he did go. Finally, he just decided to skip that painful
part and buck 'em off. Scared rider with too much
horse. Got it?"

Darby nodded. It made sense. She'd done almost

the same thing when Joker seemed about to take off, even though she'd been expecting trouble.

"This time," Jonah instructed her, "when Joker's about to buck, just press your elbows against your ribs, lean back enough to keep his head up, and drive him forward with your legs."

Elbows in. Head up. Drive with legs.

Darby understood, but it took three tries to do it right. Once, she lost her stirrup and Joker ended up going in a circle. Another time Darby lost her stirrup and slid halfway out of the saddle, before she pulled herself back up on the saddle horn. At last, she drove Joker through his buck and it worked just the way Jonah had said it would.

Only then did he let her dismount.

Her hands were already trembling when she noticed Joker's muzzle was covered with froth.

"How did I hurt his mouth?" she said, gasping.

She'd tried so hard to keep her hands light on the reins.

"You did fine," Jonah said, then pointed at Joker's mouth. "Not the bad kind of foam. Did you forget how to read horses, girl?"

Sweat dripped from Darby's forehead, down her temples, but she ignored it, focusing on the Appaloosa's eyes. They were so dark, they almost matched his disheveled forelock. Finally, though, she made out the gelding's expression.

"What's in his eyes?" Jonah prodded her.

"Mischief."

Surprised, Darby turned toward Cade. He still looked scruffy with concern, but he didn't sound that way.

"It's like, when you're nervous, you know how your mouth dries out?" Cade explained. "Well, he's not nervous. His mouth is wet. He's having fun messing with you."

"Oh, good," she managed.

"Turn Cade's trick horse over and come on up to the office, get out of the heat for a minute," Jonah said.

Why were her legs shaking now, when she and Joker were both safe? Darby put her hands on the saddle skirt for balance and leaned there a minute, swallowing against a kind of queasiness.

She hadn't heard Cade move off. He wouldn't, without Joker. That meant he had to still be standing there, watching her.

Darby pushed back and squared her shoulders. She offered him the reins with a steady hand, but she hadn't counted on the quaver in her voice as she said, "I just need a drink of water."

Cade nodded and took the reins, then replaced his hat.

"I don't let just anyone ride my horse," he said.

It was almost a compliment or almost a joke. Darby couldn't tell which.

"Well, I don't let my horse stomp just anyone,"

she said, gesturing at his open shirt and the hoofprint Hoku had scarred him with on the day of her arrival.

He gave a short laugh that reminded her of Jonah's, then pulled his shirt closed. He led Joker just a few steps before he looked back over his shoulder.

"I'm going out to gather cattle near Two Sisters. I'll keep an eye out for you and Ann."

"Do you know Ann?" Darby asked.

"Only met her once and she 'bout took my head off for trying to help her."

"But Ann's so nice," Darby protested.

Cade shrugged. "She was riding a blue-black horse full out and bareback"—Cade pointed west—"and I thought he was running away with her."

"Oh," Darby said, thinking of the day she'd slowed her pace so that Ann, with her injured leg, could keep up. She'd been insulted and pretty mad.

"She told me that Soda—that was the mare's name—was just shakin' her sillies out before some kid rode her, and I could go rescue someone who needed it." Cade's lips twisted in a self-mocking smile. "Anyway, you watch out for Pigtail Fault."

That was just like a real conversation, Darby thought as Cade and Joker walked away. And then she blushed, wondering why she'd even noticed.

Another time, Darby might think that having juice and peanut butter crackers with your grandfather sounded like a little-kid thing to do. But today she was grateful for the coolness of the office, and the food had made her feel less shaky and tired.

Jonah sat in Aunty Cathy's desk chair, peering so closely at the computer that his nose almost touched the screen.

When Darby wadded up the plastic from the crackers and threw it away, then stood up and tidied her drooping ponytail, Jonah asked, "Feel more confident?"

Darby considered his question for a few seconds. She didn't want her grandfather to think she was full of herself, but she couldn't deny she did feel more confident.

"This morning helped a lot," Darby said, "but how do you think I'm doing?"

She waited for Jonah to mention she'd ridden Joker through an aftershock. Wouldn't that be a big deal to anyone?

"Fine," he said. "But you have one more horse to go."

"Tomorrow," she reminded him.

"Why wait?" Jonah asked. "In the old days, they'd hire bronc busters who'd work through ten or fifteen colts in a day. Pretty soon, they just depended on muscle memory."

"And cruelty," Darby said. "Besides, I'm—"

She stopped short of saying she was too tired and sweaty to ride Baxter. Maybe Jonah was right. Hours of riding, reacting instead of listing steps one, two, and three, might make her responses automatic.

Still, she made one more weak protest. "Really, I think tomorrow would be better, don't you?"

"No." Jonah gave her a buddy-buddy punch in the shoulder and activated the office walkie-talkie.

"Yes, sir," Kit's voice crackled to them from someplace on the ranch.

"Bring Baxter up. I got you a bronc buster," Jonah said.

"Yes, boss. You want me to help 'er out?"

"You better. I can't bear to watch," Jonah joked. "Just let me know if we need an ambulance."

Buckin' Baxter trembled with anticipation. He sniffed Darby's boots, jeans, and hands, and Kit didn't object when she stroked the horse's blueberry-and cream-colored neck.

He shook like a big dog, allowing her to lead him around the pen as if the reins were a leash.

"What should I do?" Darby asked Kit when they rounded the last bit of the corral and stopped in front of him.

Arms crossed, Kit leaned against the fence.

"I'm more of an expert on the business of makin' 'em buck, not stoppin' 'em," Kit said. "But if I were you, I'd just get on and put him through his paces the way you did the other two."

"But I'm not one-hundredth as good a rider as Kimo," Darby said in a high-pitched whisper that caught Baxter's attention. "And Baxter bucks with him."

"Kimo'll be the first one to tell you he let Baxter get away with it too many times. You're going to catch Baxter and not give him a chance to buck with you even once," Kit told her. He stood next to the roan's head, watching her prepare to mount.

"If I get bucked off and break something, and I can't go do this project, it won't be my fault if I fail my Ecology class," Darby said.

She rested a few ounces of her weight in Baxter's left stirrup, then a little more, and slowly lifted her leg over Baxter's back. She winced at the ache in her legs before settling in the saddle.

"I don't think Jonah sets much importance on grades," Kit said, hiding his smile.

"But I do," Darby said. She let the reins flow in straight lines from her fingers to the snaffle bit rings, waiting for clues to Baxter's feelings.

"Then I guess you better not get bucked off," Kit said, and he took a step back to let her put the horse into a walk.

Twenty minutes later, Baxter still hadn't bucked. He'd been edgy, breaking a sweat instantly. He'd thrust his tongue at his bit while he moved from a walk to a jog to a lope, and Darby never stopped watching for something that might make him shy, but she didn't let herself be distracted. Finally, when Kit said "Whoa," she was amazed to see that Kimo, Jonah, and Megan all stood around the pen, watching.

"Do you know what that is?" Jonah asked.

Darby looked around before getting off Baxter. Was Jonah talking to her?

"Dumb luck?" Megan joked.

"Looks like horse mastery to me," Kit said.

"Looks like I better find a new job," Kimo complained.

As Darby dismounted, Jonah kept watching.

"That colt wanted a boss and you told him you were it. He's not going to give you any trouble because he can tell you're ready for it. No need to blush about it."

"Thank you," Darby said. She'd concentrated so hard on each sound and move of Baxter's, she felt like she'd just woken up.

"A horse can't buck, kick, or rear when he's moving forward. All bets are off if you decide to ride an outlaw, but if you keep him moving ahead, you'll usually be fine. Most horses don't want to hurt humans. If they did, we wouldn't stand a chance."

"Thank you," Darby said again.

"Come tell Mom about it," Megan encouraged Darby. "She's going nuts up there."

"She's only been in bed for a day," Jonah pointed out.

"It seems more like a week." Megan rolled her eyes. "She's sick of television, bored with magazines, and she's finished reading all of her library books."

"Okay, go visit," Jonah told Darby, "but cool this horse out and untack him first." Jonah waited until Darby nodded, then said, "Think you might want to take him instead of Navigator?"

Darby thought of Pele, of Ann's rowdy Sugarfoot, and Hoku. Trying to pony Hoku with Baxter would be insane. They'd be wrapped up in rope like bugs in a spider's web.

"No thanks." Darby barely pronounced the words before yawning. She lifted her hand in a wave and began walking.

I did it, Darby thought as she led Baxter to the tack shed.

Now, if she could just walk back to the house without doing a face plant into the dirt, it would've been a really good day.

Chapter 14

The Two Sisters wore leis of smoke on the morning the Potters were due to arrive with a four-horse trailer to pick up Darby, Megan, Hoku, and Navigator. There was no denying that the earthquake had disturbed the more active of the volcanoes, and this upset in nature only scraped nerves already made raw by the girls' plans to leave the ranch.

Jonah stood on Sun House's lanai when Darby emerged from her bedroom.

"News says our smoky skies are coming from Kilauea. It's as much from 'atmospheric conditions' as volcanic activity. The earthquake may have shaken things up, but there's no sulphur smell."

"That's good to know," Darby told him. She was

relieved to hear that the smoke was drifting from a volcano on the Big Island. "I'm about finished packing."

Jonah watched Darby with the same intensity that had made her afraid of him the day she'd arrived on Wild Horse Island. She remembered thinking that if she'd met him in the city, she would have crossed to the other side of the street.

But now he just looked like her grandfather, not some stranger with a concealed weapon, and his heavy black eyebrows, so much like her own, were lowered with . . . she wasn't sure what.

Jonah pushed away from the rail of the lanai and shook his index finger at her, but he just said, "You can breathe fine, yeah?"

"I can, but I packed my medicine just in case," Darby said.

"Okay then," Jonah said. "You better eat up and get out there. Those horses won't groom themselves."

Darby was on her way to the tack shed when Megan pounded down the stairs from her apartment. Her cherry Coke—colored ponytail bounced out the back of her baseball cap, her white T-shirt was tucked without a wrinkle into her jeans, and her full saddlebags were slung over her shoulder.

She smiled as she fell into step beside Darby, then announced, "My mom's gone nuts."

"She probably just—" Darby began.

"Totally crazy," Megan interrupted. "She told me

to go ride with you and Ann, and quit 'hovering' over her. She says she'll rest more if she's not trying to prove to me that she's fine. Tell me," Megan pleaded with melodramatic gestures, "does that make sense?"

Darby knew Megan wouldn't be chattering like this if her mother's condition was really serious, but she wasn't sure what to say.

It didn't matter, because Bart, sensing the girls' excitement, raced up and threw himself at Megan's legs.

"Bart, no." Megan dodged the Australian shepherd when he tried for a second collision, and then she went on, "And then, once I agreed to go—which I wanted to, but I was trying to be, you know, responsible—she told me not to ride Tango, because there are wild horses up there, supposedly, and they might get Tango to 'revert.'"

When Megan made quotation marks in the air, Bart hurled himself, snapping, toward her fingers.

"Bart!" Cade shouted from the tack room.

The dog wagged his stumpy tail in apology, but stayed with Megan.

"So I say, 'Fine, I'll ride Biscuit,'" Megan continued, "but when I look up from packing my stuff, Mom is staring out the window at the smoke, steam, whatever, saying she won't sleep until I get back, because there could be an eruption!"

"I bet she—"

"And I say, 'Mom, just tell me what you want me

to do,' and you know what she said?"

Darby shook her head, trying not to smile at her friend's frustration.

"She told me"—Megan paused to put her hands on her hips and lean toward Darby—"that it wasn't very nice to be rude to her when she wasn't feeling well!"

Megan whipped off her cap and threw it on the ground.

"Don't even think about it!" she threatened Bart.

Instead of retrieving the cap, the dog sat and stared at Megan with the concentration of an obedience champion.

"That's better," Megan said. "Go to Cade."

As the dog trotted off, Megan sighed, picked up her cap and shook the dust from it, and asked, "So, what are you doing?"

"Grooming Hoku and Navigator," Darby said.

"Great," Megan said, and she walked a bit faster.

"The Potters are supposed to be here in about twenty minutes," Darby added.

"The sooner, the better," Megan said.

Navigator, Hoku, and Biscuit shone from brushing by the time Jonah showed up at the tack room.

Darby and Megan met each other's eyes, hoping they weren't in for more advice.

Jonah considered the horses as he said, "You're only spending two nights. The Potters will take you to the drop-off on the road below the Two Sisters. It's about a six-mile climb to the very top. You can go as high as you like on Babe's volcano, because it's stone cold—"

"We can? I thought . . . ," Darby began, but Megan was nodding.

"But it's *kapu* past the stone trees."

Kapu. This time, the Hawaiian word gave Darby chills. It sounded less like breaking a rule and more like an unforgivable sin.

"That's only two miles away and that's close enough. Don't go up and look into the crater. It's tempting—"

"No, it's terrifying," Darby said, but when she glanced at Megan, she saw that the older girl's arms were crossed.

Megan looked totally confident, but Darby remembered that even when Tutu had told her about the Fire Maiden becoming a horse the color of flames that danced on the lava pool, she'd thought not about the spirit horse, but about the lake of molten rock.

She would not go up and look into the active volcano. No way would she expose herself or her horses to that kind of danger.

"Wouldn't it be too hot?" Darby asked suddenly. "I'm not going up there," she added, when Jonah's head snapped around and his eyes locked on her. "But don't scientists need special suits and stuff to get close enough to study a—"

Jonah didn't wait for her to finish. "I'm not crazy

about those two standing so close together," he said.

Those two . . . ? Darby thought. Even Jonah didn't have the kind of authority to make volcanoes scoot away from each other.

But Jonah jerked on Navigator's tie rope to release him and lead him away from Hoku.

The bay stepped back at his urging, and Hoku flattened her ears at Jonah.

"You keep your opinions to yourself," he told the filly.

But Darby could see Hoku was improving. A simple flicker of her ears was pretty good for a filly that hated men.

Finally, after Darby and Megan had kissed Aunty Cathy—who'd come downstairs despite Jonah's grumbling—good-bye, Darby and Jonah stood on the knoll she often used to help her mount.

Her grandfather had given her so much volcano advice, she was beginning to feel a little scared.

"If you don't think we should go," Darby blurted, "I don't have to. I've got a whole week to do something else for this project."

"Naw," Jonah made a dismissing gesture. "You've got your thick-soled boots to protect you from hot ground, and you can ride in them—besides, our lava is pretty tame, and you can depend on Megan."

The older girl flashed a shaka sign their way, but Jonah went on talking.

"The only way you get in trouble is letting its

beauty tempt you too close. Our lava's so slow-flowing, you can get mesmerized and not notice you've been cut off from the path you want to take. But you're smart. You won't stand and watch it. You'll get away while you can."

"That's right," Darby assured her grandfather.

But even when the sound of a heavy vehicle turning onto 'Iolani Ranch road made them both look up, Jonah hadn't finished.

"You'll ride up the slope from the drop-off. If there's trouble, just go back down the same way. In an emergency, if you're cut off from the road, take the lava tube down to the beach. The Boy Scouts do it every August, so it's no big secret. From that beach, you can look up and see Sun House."

Dogs barked. Truck doors slammed.

Brown skin crinkled at the corner of Jonah's eyes. He pulled Darby into a hug.

"You take it all in, then tell me about it," Jonah said.

Darby returned her grandfather's warmhearted hug, but she wasn't surprised when he let her go and looked embarrassed by his kindness.

He squeezed her arm with a work-callused hand, and said, "Don't let that *pupule* mustang get you into trouble."

When he strode over to greet the Potters, Darby tagged along behind him, still grinning.

* * *

An hour later, they'd almost reached the drop-off where the Potters would help the girls unload their gear and horses.

Darby liked Ann's parents. Mr. Potter had red hair sprinkled with gray, and Mrs. Potter wore her sparrow-brown hair in a braid. Tanned, middle-aged, and happy, the Potters told Darby to call them Ed and Ramona.

Besides Ann, they had a shy seven-year-old named Toby and a baby called Buck. Both boys were strapped into the extended cab of their truck. Darby, Megan, and Ann had had to fit themselves in where they could.

"Hey, Megan, how's the team going to do this season?" Mr. Potter asked, reminding Darby that Ann and Megan had been soccer teammates.

"It'll do," Megan said, "but we miss Ann."

"Yeah," Ann huffed, as if she blamed her parents, not her injury, for her removal from the team.

Darby didn't blame her. Ann's soccer skills were so excellent, she'd been the only eighth grader ever to compete on the Lehua High School team.

Ann's mother didn't let her dwell on the injustice of her accident.

"Ann, can you distract Toby from sucking his thumb? I don't know why he's back at it."

Toby pressed his face into Ann's shoulder. She stroked his head and planted a kiss on the nape of his neck.

"And Darby, if Buck is bothering you, just tell him no," Mrs. Potter said when she noticed the little boy cooing as he threaded his finger through Darby's long black hair.

"He's fine," Darby told her. As an only child, she'd never felt the chubby, exploring hand of a baby, and she kind of liked it.

"I should mention that his real name is Buchanan. That's my maiden name," she said.

"Buck is a good old Nevada name," Mr. Potter protested.

"I just can't get over the fact that your little mustang's a Nevadan, too," Mrs. Potter said. "I do miss seeing the Calico Mountains from my kitchen window." She patted her husband's shoulder before adding, "But I don't miss deep snow or pushing hay bales off a flatbed truck while Ed sat in the cozy truck cab with the heater on full blast."

"It was never that way," Mr. Potter assured Darby, then added, "Well, almost never."

Then the smile faded from his face. "You say Shan Stonerow had your filly." Mr. Potter pronounced the name as if it was bitter in his mouth. "That good-for-nothing—"

"Dear," Mrs. Potter cautioned her husband.

"Some folks don't deserve good horses."

"*Any* horses," Ann put in.

"Sam Forster faxed me his phone number, in case I wanted to get in touch with him," Darby said.

"Don't waste your time. If Hoku was his, you're lucky she's not ruined. He rode all his stock young. Yearlings, I'm talkin' about, and he beat the devil out of them. At least that's how he put it."

They drove for about five minutes before Mr. Potter said, "I don't know if I've ever been so mad at my dad as I was the day he sold this grulla colt of ours to Stonerow. Dad got it into his head that the colt was bad luck. He was a jumper. And fast? Let me tell you, kids, he could punch a hole in the wind and run right through it."

Mr. Potter looked up into his rearview mirror and Darby met his eyes as he asked, "She have scars on her face? No? Well then, maybe she got the better of him. Wouldn't that be something."

Mr. Potter's grin got bigger as he mulled over the possibility.

A few miles later, as the road turned steep, Mr. Potter chuckled and shook his head. "Still hard for me to believe Wyatt married a woman from the Bureau of Land Management. The Wyatt Forster I remember had no use for the bureau or wild horses, but I guess times do change. Hey now, we should give this lady a hand."

The girls leaned around Buck and Toby, seeking a better view out the windows.

"I don't recognize her, do you?" Mrs. Potter asked. "Ann?"

"Nope," Ann said.

"Megan?"

Megan removed her cap as if it obscured her view, then said, "Me either."

Darby's eyes tracked the dotted yellow line down the center of the street until she saw the woman at the roadside. She wore a stylish red dress and red high heels, but somehow managed to look at home in this desolate place.

As Mr. Potter steered the truck and trailer carefully off the road, stopping out of traffic, Darby saw the woman push a cloud of curly black hair back from her face. Her features were those of a warrior queen, and she stood in a column of smoke.

Darby's chest went tight, and it had nothing to do with asthma.

Red is her color, black is her hair. Respect Fire Maiden, or I warn you: beware.

"Car must've overheated coming up this hill," Mr. Potter said.

Darby saw the red Miata convertible the woman leaned against. Of course it was steam, not a column of smoke, that rolled out from under the car's propped-up hood.

As Mr. Potter left the truck and offered to help the stranded motorist, Darby kicked herself for being so gullible. Her imagination had rarely conjured up magical people and situations when she lived in Pacific Pinnacles.

So what if she was in Hawaii now? Pele did not drive a red convertible.

As they lowered the windows to listen, they heard Mr. Potter say, "Let me get a rag or something to take this cap off so we can add some water. No, ma'am, you don't want to do that with your bare hands. It's over two hundred degrees. I'll be right back."

Mr. Potter looked puzzled as he walked back toward the truck. The woman's laughter floated after him.

"Everything okay?" Mrs. Potter asked as her husband rummaged around on the truck's floor.

"Why she'd laugh about gettin' her fingerprints burnt off, I don't know," Mr. Potter grumbled.

"Is she a tourist?" Mrs. Potter asked.

"I guess." Mr. Potter picked up a piece of cloth and folded it as he said, "She wants to see 'the top blow off a mountain,' is what she said. When I mentioned for her to be careful, since they spew out millions of pounds of lava a minute, she laughed at that, too. Woman must have the brains of a grasshopper."

"Don't say that!" Darby blurted.

The entire family stared at her. Toby's thumb fell out of his mouth.

Darby couldn't explain that Pele would send them up in flames for their lack of respect, so she just stared at the window, feeling awful.

"Sorry, Darby, you're right," Mr. Potter said. "Probably just standing in the heat like this has got her head a bit addled."

"She—" Darby pointed and gasped. The metal lid

of something under the car's hood, maybe the radiator, dropped from the woman's hand, struck the pavement, and rolled on its edge until Mr. Potter ran around the front of the red car and blocked it with his boot.

Mrs. Potter jumped out to give first aid, and Ann said, "She did it. But she couldn't have. She's not screaming."

As the Potters fussed around the woman, Megan elbowed Ann and asked, "You know who she looks like?"

"Who?"

"Check her out," Megan insisted. "You've been on a field trip to the museum, right?"

"Yeah, but I don't know . . ." Ann concentrated. "Not a queen."

"Pele!" Megan whispered, underlining Darby's fear.

"Megan, come on," Ann said in a long-suffering tone.

"I'm just sayin', we all saw her take that hot thing out from under the hood—"

The woman in red looked calmly toward the truck.

"Is she looking at us, Annie?" Toby asked.

At the little boy's fearful tone, Darby sat up straighter and Megan cleared her throat.

"Uh-huh," Ann said, and then, casting around for an excuse to satisfy her little brother, she said, "She probably doesn't think we all look related."

"That's for sure," Darby blurted.

Megan twisted in her seat, ending up nearly nose to nose with Darby.

"We could be sisters. We have the same eyebrows and eyes, practically the same mouth, and my hair's just got more red in it than yours," Megan said as if she'd given it some thought. Then she turned to point at Ann. "Not quite as much red as yours."

While Ann and Megan laughed, Darby enjoyed a surge of delight. She'd been about to dispute Megan's compliment—and whether Megan knew it or not, that's what it was—by saying Megan looked like a fashion model and she looked like a soft, pale grub.

But something kept Darby from saying it. Probably, she thought, she just wanted Megan's opinion to be true.

"What?" Megan said, as if she felt Darby's eyes on her.

"You'd be a great big sister," Darby admitted.

For a second, Megan looked touched, but then she flounced back in her seat, crossed her arms, and said, "I know it."

Toby was naming Megan's hair color, then Darby's and Ann's, when Darby's gaze turned to the woman at the roadside. Darby agreed with Toby. There was something calculating in the woman's expression, as if she were memorizing them.

Just remember we stopped to help you, Darby sent her

thoughts toward the woman, even though she couldn't possibly be the ancient fire goddess.

After a few more endless minutes, the woman got into her car and started the engine. She signed okay to the Potters and Mr. Potter slammed her sports car's hood. The lady in red waved as she roared away from them.

With their heads close together, Ann's parents were definitely talking about the strange woman, but once they were back in the car, Mrs. Potter just smiled and said, "She used the hem of that lovely silk dress to protect her hand while she unscrewed the radiator cap."

"Oh," Ann, Darby, and Megan said together, and when Toby and Buck echoed them, everyone laughed.

Chapter 15

The Potters had driven away from the drop-off point, with its water spigot, bulletin board, and sign-in sheet, about an hour before.

Darby rode Navigator and led Hoku up the Two Sisters slope at a slow and steady pace. Both horses were interested in the steep terrain and unfamiliar place, but they moved with a calm cooperation Darby could barely believe.

"They're doing great," Megan said, and soon she'd lost her frown and fallen into the role of tour guide for the two mainland girls.

Rocking with Biscuit's smooth gait, Megan pointed out ohia trees with bright red blooms. When she called them Pele's trees, she sounded matter-of-fact, not superstitious.

"What's that bird?" Darby asked.

The girls drew rein and listened.

"The one that sounds like you're changing stations on an old dial radio? That one?" Ann asked as the bird called again.

"Yeah," Darby said.

"I'm not sure," Megan said, still listening.

"I have no idea." Ann sounded a little stiff to Darby.

In fact, she'd sounded that way ever since they'd unloaded the horses, and Darby had a pretty good idea why.

"I didn't mean to snap at your dad," Darby said.

"Then why did you?" The corners of Ann's lips turned down as if she was hurt, but not angry.

"You'll think I'm dumb. Dumber than a grasshopper," Darby joked "But I'll tell you, because I don't want to wreck our —"

"Just tell me!"

Darby took a deep breath, then said, "It was — what Megan said."

"Pele?" Ann and Megan said together.

"Look, I'm just learning about these legends —"

"Stories," Megan substituted.

"Stories," Darby repeated, "and it was on my mind because of our project. I was thinking that since we're in her territory and she demands respect and the way that woman was looking at us kind of got me . . . what?"

"Nothing," Ann said.

"You gave me a weird smile," Darby said. She glanced at Megan, who looked more rigid in the saddle than usual.

"Oh, it's nothing. I would have told you before if I thought you were worrying, " Ann teased.

Darby reined Navigator closer, so they were stirrup to stirrup. Finally, Ann admitted, "When you were unloading Hoku, my mom told me that the woman told her she'd been looking at me because she loved my hair."

"That's okay, then," Darby said, feeling better for a few seconds.

"Because red is her favorite color . . . ," Megan said in a spooky voice.

"That's right, harass the new girl," Darby said, controlling the urge to stick out her tongue at her friends, "but gods and goddesses are famous for changing into things, right? And Tutu says that Pele can change into the Fire Maiden—"

"Who?" Ann asked.

"An amazing golden horse."

"I've never heard that," Ann said.

"I have," Megan admitted. "The wild horses up here are supposed to be sacred to Pele, but I've never seen one."

As they rode, Darby retold Tutu's tale of the white stallion who was really Pele's brother, the god of steam, and the black stallion who was another brother, the god of thunderclouds.

"I knew about the battle between Pele and the sea goddess. Fire and water constantly fighting each other," Ann mused. "I always sort of thought the Two Sisters were named for them."

"They are," Megan said.

Darby stared at the cones on the horizon. She couldn't believe she hadn't thought of that when Tutu had been telling her story, but of course that made sense.

The girls had admired each other's horses while unloading them, but they didn't get a real chance to study them until they stopped in the shade to eat their sandwiches.

Sugarfoot was a caramel-and-cream-colored pinto. As he grazed on the plants sprouting from the volcanic dirt, his two-toned mane touched the ground.

"He looks so sweet," Darby said.

"Why can't you use him as a therapy horse?" Megan asked.

"Sugarfoot's a chaser," Ann confessed.

"A chaser?" Darby asked, and she noticed Megan stopped chewing her sandwich and raised her eyebrows as if she wasn't sure what Ann meant, either.

"It's a vice you don't hear about a lot, because people are ashamed to admit they're afraid of their own horses. That's my theory, anyway."

"What does he chase?" Darby asked.

"Anything that runs from him. People, dogs, cars. It's more common in stallions, but he came so close to hurting one of our adult clients, it was scary. The guy was out in our pasture in his wheelchair, and Shug came galloping at him. He's a Morab—half Morgan and half Arabian—but when he charges, you can imagine some sheikh with a spear riding him into battle." Ann pretended to shiver. "He looks fierce. So our client took off, and Shug chased him and knocked him over. The metal wheelchair kind of protected him. If he hadn't been in it, he would have been hurt for sure. My dad wanted to get rid of Sugarfoot on the spot—"

"You can bet Jonah would have," Megan said.

"—but it's a colt thing, and he's outgrowing it. Plus, my mom and I have worked with him a lot."

"Wow," Darby said, looking at the horse differently now. "Why does he do it?"

"He's playing," Ann said. Then, in the tone of a parent admitting a child's flaw, she added, "And he hasn't tried it for three months, but if he ever did, with either of you—"

"Don't back down?" Megan guessed.

"Right," Ann said. "Stand your ground, and when he gets close, like a few car lengths away, start jumping up and down and waving your arms like crazy."

"Does that work?" Darby asked.

"No, but it's fun to watch," Megan put in.

"Yes, it works. He comes to a screeching halt,

shoots you a dirty look, and starts poking around for something to eat," Ann told them.

Darby felt relieved by Ann's description of the young gelding's disappointment when people wouldn't play his game, but she wondered what would happen if they came upon any wild horses.

"Let's go, so we'll have time to explore the lava tube before dark," Megan said, crumpling up her lunch sack.

Ann shoved things back in her pack, too.

"You've got flashlights, don't you?" Megan asked.

"Sure," Ann said.

"Jonah made me bring one," Darby said.

"Cool. We'll make camp when we get to the stone trees, put up our stakeout line, and go ahead on foot."

"Okay," Darby agreed, but she couldn't help thinking that the thing had been formed by lava. That meant it was a known path for the flow of molten rock on its way downhill.

She'd hate for Ann and Megan to think she was a coward, but it was probably best to confess her worries now.

"Brock, brock," she said.

Both her friends laughed out loud and Hoku snorted with pricked ears.

"Was that a chicken sound?" Ann asked.

"I'm not real excited about going into the lava tube," Darby admitted.

"It's not creepy and tight around you, like a cave,"

Megan said. "Our lava tube has a twelve-foot ceiling and it's almost that wide. You can ride a horse in there."

"Shoot, you could probably ride an elephant in there," Ann joked.

"A small elephant," Megan corrected.

Swallowing hard, Darby looked up at the cone-shaped peak. Being in confined spaces didn't scare her, but curtains of flame and rivers of molten rock did.

"The ohia trees," Ann said, pointing as they rode on. "It looks like they get scarcer closer to the top of the volcanoes. Is that because of the heat?"

Darby noticed the trees had fewer red blooms nearer the top, too, and they looked more fragile than the ones around them here.

"Yeah," Megan said.

"The thing that's weird to me," Ann went on, "is that the tree and its flower have different names. I mean, that's like a rosebush having tulips blooming on it, isn't it?"

It crossed Darby's mind that Ann might be trying to distract her from her fear, and she smiled.

"It's because of that story," Megan said. "Pele fell in love with a youth named Ohia . . ."

Youth, Darby thought, and her smile grew wider. Megan's voice shifted into that of a storyteller, and Darby wondered if she'd heard this tale from her father.

"Ohia was already betrothed—engaged," Megan said to them, "and even though he knew it was dangerous, he refused Pele's love.

"You know Pele has a hot temper, so she turned him into a tree, but not just any tree. It was one she could always keep around her, one that could close its pores when the sulphur gas came from the volcano, and even if it does die from the heat or lava, it's the first tree to grow back after an eruption."

"So, she kept him with her, whether he wanted to be or not," Ann said.

"Yeah, but after Pele did Ohia's makeover," Megan said, "his girlfriend Lehua came around looking for him. Pele told her the truth, and Lehua's heart was broken. She couldn't stop crying. So Pele took pity on her and turned her into a flower—which had to be red, of course, since that's Pele's favorite color—and Pele placed her on the Ohia tree. So they would be together forever."

"That was kind of nice of her," Darby said.

Megan paused in her story as a hot wind blasted down the slope they were ascending.

Darby saw Biscuit and Sugarfoot close their eyes against the dust and felt Navigator's walk turn more cautious. She looked back over her shoulder to see Hoku lift her head and flare her nostrils. Maybe there was a new smell on the wind.

"Pele also discourages you from picking lehua blooms to make a lei or anything," Megan explained.

"You can do it, but you'll start a rainstorm. Lehua still cries when she's taken from Ohia."

"We're definitely putting that in our report," Ann said. "Especially that part about the pores and the sulphur. Science and story coming together. That is too cool."

As they rode under a tree so heavily laden with lehua flowers that they brushed the girls' hair, Ann looked at Darby with an impish grin and reached her hand up.

"Shall we see if we can really start a rainstorm?"

"No." Darby tried to keep the uneasiness out of her voice.

"I didn't know you were so superstitious," Ann said, but she lowered her arm without disturbing the flowers.

"It's not superstition," Megan corrected. "It's respect for our heritage."

"I didn't mean . . ." Ann blushed and looked down at her saddle horn.

"Crusher," Megan's voice was affectionate as she used Ann's soccer nickname, "I know you didn't mean to—but that's one of those—wait." Megan held her hand out in a halt sign and for a full minute, she looked thoughtful. "You know how Ty got up in your face about Pele?"

Darby and Ann nodded together.

"He overreacts, but I think he's just trying to sort out what he believes about ancient customs and stuff like that." Megan shrugged. "I've already figured out what I think. I'm just respectful. That's all."

"Okay, Meggie," Ann said. "I'm taking you for my role model, even if I'm not Hawaiian."

"Me too," Darby said, "even if I'm only—"

"Knock it off, you guys," Megan said, rolling her eyes at their admiration. "Keep your horses on the path. We're almost to the place where we'll, uh, set up camp."

When Megan's voice faltered, Darby straightened in the saddle and looked ahead.

She saw the strange stone trees, and on the ground below them, a scarlet scattering of lehua blossoms from a pair of ohia trees.

Chapter 16

Darby's surprise must have traveled all the way down the tangerine-and-white-striped lead rope to Hoku, because the filly began skittering and shying.

"No big deal, you guys," Megan said, and when both younger girls stayed silent, she added jokingly, "Listen to your big sister. Obviously, it was the wind."

Darby felt the same little bounce of pleasure she had when Megan proposed sisterhood before, but she just nodded.

About half of the blossoms blew away as the girls set up the horses' highline.

They tied each end of a long rope to the ohia trees.

It looked like a clothesline, Darby thought.

They watered and hand-grazed the horses, then put neck ropes on them and tied each one individually to the long rope, making sure the horses were spaced apart and didn't have enough slack to get a leg over the rope.

Hands on her hips, Megan surveyed their work.

"That should hold them, unless all four work together to pull down the trees," she said.

"Or a herd of wild horses charges through," Darby said.

"I've seen tracks up here, but no horses," Megan said. "And since no one around here shoes their horses, the tracks could have been from domestic ones."

Darby watched Hoku. Quiet again, the filly ignored her neck rope to survey the area. She didn't act like there was a wild herd nearby.

"Remember, though," Darby said to Megan, "when Black Lava showed up on 'Iolani and Kit chased him off? He said he headed them through the fold, in this direction, so that they wouldn't go back toward Crimson Vale and Manny."

Ann made a disapproving noise.

"Yeah, and Kimo said there used to be wild horses up here," Megan said.

"The stories had to come from somewhere," Darby said.

"Hey!" Ann clapped her hands to get the other girls' attention. "I need one of my mom's candy-bar brownies to build up my energy for exploring. Wanna share?"

Ann burrowed into her backpack and unwrapped the sweets. Darby and Ann leaned against the stone trees, eating, while Megan searched the area for a twig to use as a pencil. Then she drew a diagram in the dirt while the other girls watched.

First, Megan drew a wild flow of lines descending from a volcano.

"This is pahoehoe lava," Megan said, "the kind that looks more . . ."

"Smooth," Darby said, "not the spiky *a'a'* stuff."

One of the first things Darby had learned about Hawaii was its two kinds of lava—smooth pahoehoe and rough *a'a'*.

"Right," Megan said, like an approving teacher. "Well, pahoehoe hardens on top, but lava underneath keeps running for a while, and makes it to the beach, over on the north shore where the water is rough and cold. And then . . . ker-splash!"—Megan slashed geyser-shaped lines sprouting up from the waves she'd drawn—"All the hot lava goes into the sea, leaving this kind of lava shell that you can walk through. That's a lava tube."

"The only thing I'm worried about is it gets wet in there sometimes," Ann said.

Megan's gaze darted to Ann's injured knee.

"The flashlights should pick up the shine of any

water. We'll be careful. Promise."

Darby watched the horses as she packed her fanny pack with her flashlight, water, inhaler, and a granola bar.

Hoku seemed strangely at ease.

Could the cone-shaped volcanoes remind the mustang of the Calico Mountains? Samantha Forster had mentioned that the Phantom's herd of wild horses had galloped into a tunnel through the mountains.

Darby didn't know much about Nevada geography and geology, but she supposed it could be something like this.

The lava tube turned out to be an hour hike from camp.

"Stay on the path," Megan reminded them as they walked toward the lava tube, but she also pointed out interesting landmarks, like a lava formation that looked like lions' paws, but was really lava that had hardened before it got very far.

"That's Pele's hair and tears," Megan said, pointing to the right side of the path. "Don't step on them."

When lava was flung into the air, tiny beads of it became glassy comets. Most shattered when they hit the ground, Megan explained, but some broke apart and the "comets'" heads became Pele's tears, while the tails became Pele's hair.

"When we get inside, I'll show you Pele's tears,"

Megan said. "Shine your flashlights up on the ceiling, and you'll see them. They look like baby stalactites, but they're hollow, made by the river of lava melting the ceiling."

"Our big sister knows everything," Darby teased, and then Ann grabbed her hand and they skipped after Megan as if they were kindergartners.

"You guys"—Megan was laughing as she looked over her shoulder at them—"be sure—"

"To stay on the path," the girls chanted together.

Darby felt giddy with delight. This new part of her Hawaiian home was amazing.

The girls kept walking until they came to a steam vent.

"I've seen one of these before," Darby said. "Not far from the *kipuka*."

A crack in the earth yawned open, its lips powdered with yellow sulphur, like the mouth of a messy eater.

"That's Pigtail Fault, isn't it?" Ann asked.

"It is? Cade told me about it, but I thought it was just like a crack." Darby peered into the opening. The bright yellow at the surface shaded to a peachy color the deeper she looked, and heat snakes wavered everywhere.

Megan was strangely silent, surveying the terrain around them until Ann asked again, "Is it Pigtail Fault?"

"It is," she admitted.

"It was closed, just a crack, when I saw it before," Ann said.

"They change," Megan said, walking on, but Darby would bet they were all three wondering if the earthquake had shaken it open wider.

When they reached the opening of the lava tube, Darby's bravery had wilted a bit. It was a good thing Ann and Megan couldn't see inside her imagination, because it held a fearful image of them running down the lava tube with a scalding flood of molten rock chasing after them.

"I'll go first," Ann offered. She whirled her flashlight over her head like she was wielding a cutlass, advancing into battle.

As soon as she disappeared, Darby felt the urge to follow, and it wasn't fear of being left alone. She didn't want to be left out.

"Me next?" she asked. Megan made an after-you gesture, and Darby followed her flashlight's beam into the dark.

As soon as they stepped inside, the coolness and scent reminded Darby of Black Lava's hiding place behind the Crimson Vale waterfall.

She smelled wet stone and animals, and something else.

"Don't you love this?" Ann's voice echoed.

"Yeah," Darby said. "I really do!"

She stepped along carefully behind Ann, engulfed by the elation of being in a secret place. She heard the whisper of far-off waves. Leaning her head back, she spotlighted smooth globes that had once dripped like wax.

"I would have named them Pele's pearls," Darby said.

And Megan murmured, "Nice."

"Water's dripped from the roof." Ann's echo came back to them from farther down the tunnel.

"Watch your step," Megan called.

"I will," Ann shouted back, but just then she yelped.

For an instant, Darby held her ears against the echo, but then she let her hands drop and she could hear Ann breathing heavily.

"What's wrong?" Darby saw whirling brightness. It must be Ann's flashlight making crazy shadows all around them.

"What was that about?" Megan asked, stepping past Darby to hurry after Ann.

Darby lengthened her stride. She wasn't really afraid, but there was something about being the last one in line that gave her the creeps.

Ann had slipped on a smooth, wet piece of the lava-rock floor, but she was already back on her feet when Darby saw something black sweep through the air.

Or maybe she'd just blinked. Darby wasn't sure.

"Are there bats in here?" she asked.

"What do I look like, the Discovery Channel?"

Megan grumbled, but there was a hint of worry in her tone as she said, "My dad always said Hawaii had no cave bats, only tree bats."

"Bats don't really dive into your hair," Ann protested.

"Who said they did?" Megan still sounded edgy.

"And they're mammals," Darby put in, "like dogs and—"

"I like my mammals without wings, thank you," Megan said.

They giggled as all three flashlight beams joined together, searching cracks in the lava around them, but they didn't see anything on the rock ceiling except trailing roots that had forced through from the surface.

Navigator neighed a welcome when he saw the girls coming back to camp.

Sugarfoot came as close to Ann as his tie rope would allow.

Hoku vibrated with alertness, ears pricked toward the summit of Two Sisters.

Biscuit looked like a giraffe. His neck strained against his rope, and when he looked back guiltily, he was chewing, his usually black muzzle purple.

"What have you got?" Megan asked, stepping ahead of Ann and Darby.

Dozens of berries that looked like a cross between cranberries and coffee beans were scattered around him. Some rolled in reach of the other horses, but they weren't interested.

"'Ohelo berries?" Ann said.

"Of course," Megan said, "although I thought only goats ate them." Megan took Biscuit's muzzle in her hands and looked into his brown eyes. "Not a good idea, Biscuit."

The buckskin swished his tail, pulled his head away from Megan, and looked around for more berries.

Darby squatted to examine them.

"Tutu told me they're Pele's favorites," Darby said. She could see her reflection in the berries' reddish sheen. "Just hope he offered some to Pele before he ate them."

Bending from the waist, Megan plucked off a few 'ohelo berries and placed them on a nearby rock.

"He has now," she said. Then she looked at Darby. "You should try one. They're good."

Darby hesitated.

"Maybe later," she said.

"We've got plenty of food," Ann added.

While Megan moved Biscuit away from the berries, but still only a few yards from the other horses, Darby and Ann finished setting up their camp. They spread out a ground cloth, then took the rolled sleeping bags from behind the saddles they'd already stripped from the horses.

"Are we going to arrange rocks in a circle for a

fire ring?" Ann asked.

"We don't have anything that needs to be cooked," Megan said, "and if our main goal is to see the wild horses, I don't think it's a good idea. It seems like the smell of smoke would drift farther than our human scent, don't you think?"

Ann nodded.

"Now I kind of wish we'd brought the lantern," Darby said.

"We have our flashlights, and plenty of batteries," Ann told her.

"Yeah, and if we see the horses, we'll have a cool connection to the Fire Maiden story that Tutu told me," Darby agreed.

"Let's eat now," Megan said. "When the sun goes down, it's like someone turned off the lights. It's way dark," Ann said.

Darby measured out grain they'd brought for the horses, Megan fed them, and Ann set out dinner for humans—a feast of cashews, plums, salami, cheese, and water.

They were in their sleeping bags by the time darkness fell. No insects buzzed or birds called. Wind strummed the branches, and the horses shifted drowsily.

Lulled by bedding down near the horses, Darby was almost asleep when Ann said, "In the morning, we'd better make some notes."

"Umm-hmm," Darby said.

"And then let's hike up the cold sister and look for mustangs," Ann added.

"Okay," Darby answered through a yawn.

"I think we should leave our horses here, don't you?"

"Sure," Darby said.

She heard her friend turn in her sleeping bag and say, "I've never been up here at night."

But Darby didn't have the strength to raise her eyelids.

Darby woke once during the night, unsure of where she was. She'd been dreaming that she was staring into a campfire, hypnotized by a face she saw there.

She turned over in her sleeping bag and Hoku must have heard her stir, because the filly gave a gentle nicker.

Darby smiled into the darkness. Warm and comfortable, she was surprised when she was able to distinguish the volcano from the blackness all around.

Veins of gold glimmered near the top.

"What do you think? Is it lit from inside? Or are those streams of lava?"

Darby heard herself speak, but she wasn't sure whether she was talking to the other girls or to Hoku.

Finally, her pounding heart slowed down.

She must be dreaming.

Chapter 17

In the morning, Ann's leg reminded her of all the hiking she'd done yesterday, and her fall in the lava tube.

Darby wasn't surprised when Ann grumbled about the holdup, but agreed with the other girls that it made more sense to make their notes now and delay their hike to look for wild horses until later.

"I guess you guys are right. I don't want my parents grounding me from something else fun," Ann said, but then she surprised Darby by asking, "Is your asthma okay?"

"Fine."

Smoke hung in the air, and she'd taken a precautionary spray from her inhaler, but she didn't think Ann had noticed.

"Hey," Darby said, then, "What if we take Navigator for you to ride? Even if we see wild horses, I think he'll be okay."

"Sure, we'll walk and lead," Megan said.

"No way," Ann told them.

Darby crossed her arms and gave Ann a serious look.

"If I tweaked my leg, would you let me ride while you walked?" Darby was pretty sure she had Ann in a corner.

"No, we'd ride double," Ann said smugly.

When the time came to give it a try, Megan set off on foot, letting Darby and Ann have the first turn on Navigator.

Darby went along with Ann's idea to save Navigator the extra weight of the saddle by riding bareback.

"I don't think I can stay on, though," Darby said. "I might pull you off with me, and then your leg will be even worse."

"You'll get used to it really fast," Ann promised. "I'll sit in front and hold the reins, and you just hang on around my waist. You have great balance. It'll be easy."

"I don't know," Darby said, but after they'd convinced Navigator to stop prancing and showing off because they'd taken him and left Hoku, Biscuit, and Sugarfoot behind, riding double was really pretty fun.

✳ ✳ ✳

They'd cut the distance from camp to the quiet volcano's crater in half when Darby spotted something moving behind a screen of ohia trees.

It was Megan, finger held in front of her lips, so the other girls would be quiet. Then Darby saw why.

Horses!

Ann must have felt Darby's reaction, because she turned a few inches before Darby clamped her right hand over her friend's mouth. Wild-eyed, Ann turned even farther, trying to jerk her head away, until she saw Darby mouth the word *horses*.

The herd was still about a mile away, but they had to be mustangs. This land belonged to Babe and neither she nor Jonah let horses run free up here.

Ann pointed to a bulge of rock up higher, above the horses. Megan nodded and began scaling the approach to it, while Ann reined Navigator closer.

Before they got far, Black Lava appeared.

Ann sat back so quickly, Darby was afraid that they'd both tumble off backward.

The stallion was in a dangerous mood. Dark and dusty, he struck at the dirt with one feathered front leg. He was insulted by the invasion of the girls and gelding. He exposed his teeth and tossed his head with flattened ears, telling them so.

Navigator didn't need a second warning. He was taller than the stallion. He outweighed him by hundreds of pounds. Just the same, it would not be a fight of equals. Primitive entitlement—to the mares, to this spot, to this island—shone in Black Lava's eyes.

Navigator backed away from the stallion so quickly, he misjudged the slope and stumbled.

Ann slumped forward, holding onto Navigator's neck, and Darby held on to her as the huge gelding planted his hooves and managed to stay upright.

Once he was out of sight of the stallion, Navigator answered Ann's reining, carrying the girls up behind the lava outcropping she'd spotted before. Megan crouched up there, as still as part of the rock.

A pulpit of pahoehoe, Darby thought. It would be perfect for looking down on the wild herd if they stuck around.

The girls dismounted, signaling their awe and excitement with widened eyes, but staying quiet as Megan gestured for them to come on up.

Ann tied Navigator with patient, careful knots. Then Ann and Darby climbed the lava formation and hid.

Looking down, they had a good view of the wild horses.

Megan held up all of her fingers, folded them down, then held up her index finger.

Darby was puzzled until she saw that Black Lava had eleven herd members. Ann verified the count with her own fingers. There were at least three foals, maybe a fourth.

They were a rainbow of colors. One dun was the bright yellow of the sulphur at the edge of Pigtail Fault, and a small bay looked like satiny mahogany. Three grays, from charcoal to nearly white, grazed side by side, and if their leader's pacing made them nervous, they gave no sign of it.

On the outskirts of the herd stood the lead mare, and she was magnificent.

Ann leaned close to Darby and whispered, "Steel-dust." Megan gave a faint nod.

Darby guessed that was the mare's color—a pewter gray flecked with black—but her coat wasn't the mare's most outstanding quality. Her black tail almost reached the ground. Her mane rippled in ringlets down to her shoulder. Her forelock hung between her eyes, making twirling black snakes down to her nostrils.

Like the stallion and many of the other horses, wispy hair showed on her trim legs, indicating that she had draft blood. Her attention was fixed on two young horses—a putty-colored dun with a dorsal stripe and barred front legs and a bay with four white stockings.

They were definitely in time-out, Darby thought. While the mare watched, the young horses didn't dare move.

Darby thought that if the mare was hers to name, she'd call her Medusa, for the mythological Gorgon who'd had snakes in place of hair and a gaze so fearful, it transformed people to stone.

The mare turned her tail on the two colts, but each time they made a move to rejoin the herd or wander off the slope, she whirled to glare at them and they froze.

Darby wondered what the two horses could have done to deserve confinement in the lead mare's invisible penalty box.

All at once, Darby realized the sky had darkened. Had they watched the wild horses for so long, dusk was falling?

It couldn't be, Darby thought. It was still so hot. Getting hotter all the time, actually.

She looked skyward, wondering if the smoke from Kilauea had blown in and blotted out the sun, just making it feel like night was approaching.

Suddenly, Black Lava and his lead mare threw their heads high, testing the air. It wasn't smoke that had caught their attention.

Megan pointed.

A white stallion was picking his way down from the crater top of the dead volcano, right toward the herd.

"Oh my gosh," Ann gasped.

Darby expected the stallion to race in and try to steal some of Black Lava's mares, but he didn't. When Black Lava trotted out to meet him with his neck arched, the two stallions made what seemed like a civilized greeting, prancing parallel to each other, then turning and repeating the dance back in the other direction.

The four-stockinged bay slipped past the lead mare and headed toward the two stallions. He was closer now and Darby could see that the bay was marked up with bites. He was probably about to be kicked out of the herd to become a bachelor.

But that didn't mean his father would let him join up with a challenger.

Distracted by the bay's audacity, Black Lava swung on him with bared teeth.

Seeing his opening, the white stallion ran toward the herd, head swinging from side to side in a herding gesture. He was clearly intent on the lead mare.

With the bay colt in retreat, Black Lava spun around, ears flat, neck arched. He bolted toward the white stallion and stopped about ten feet away from him. Standing in a dust cloud made by his own sudden stop, the white stallion struck out with a raised foreleg.

Black Lava did the same. They each threatened, but neither wanted to fight.

Seeing the bay colt returning, the white stallion tossed his head, as if urging the youngster to defy his leader and come along. Black Lava wasn't having it. His rear was spectacular, like something you'd see in a circus, Darby thought, and then he lashed out his hind legs, nearly knocking the colt off his feet.

A black-and-white mare, brindled by shadows,

saw her chance to make a break for it. While her sisters grazed, she darted downhill.

"Where did she come from?" Ann whispered.

Medusa was after her, giving her a savage bite just above the tail, and the brindled mare stopped, ears pricked toward the other volcano.

For a second the stallions stopped their posturing, and looked in the same direction. But the lead mare bullied the black-and-white horse back, and Black Lava began pacing the boundaries of his herd. His blue eye glittered as he made a barricade with his body.

The white stallion wasn't impressed. Briefly, he flattened his ears and head, looking like a snake ready to strike. When Black Lava stopped to consider what he should do next, the white circled around and touched noses with Medusa.

Outraged, Black Lava pursued the white stallion. Mouth open, black nose stretching for the white tail, he chased the other stallion around the band until a loud explosion rocked the horses, girls, and lava-rock pulpit.

Ohia trees snapped from side to side. One even toppled to the ground.

The girls saw a crack fracture the face of the volcano directly across from them.

Before they could move, the crack grew wider. Lava welled up through it, making a red-orange fountain, and then it went down and vanished as if it had sealed itself back up.

"We've gotta get out of here!" Ann clambered down ahead of Darby, and Megan followed.

"Navigator—"

"Still there, but he's—"

"—going crazy!"

Megan jumped the last few yards to the ground, landing ahead of Darby and Ann, in front of the brown gelding. He rolled his eyes white and snorted, and Megan had just grabbed his reins below the bit when there was a tumult of hooves.

Black Lava and the steeldust mare stampeded down the slope, as if they were heading for the road.

The white stallion galloped uphill, found no escape, and now he was headed back down, right at them.

Navigator screamed. Did he want to join the white stallion's headlong run? Far in the distance, did he hear other horses answer?

"Get down!" Darby shrieked, because she'd just figured out the white stallion's plan.

Running full out, he touched on the edge of the lava pulpit and launched himself at the path they'd taken up. Darby and Ann ducked, tumbling and falling with their arms crossed over their heads, but the stallion's leap cleared them easily.

Stabbing his forelegs at the earth for balance, he shook a torrent of white mane, gathered himself, and ran past Navigator, crossing the volcano's face.

In the few seconds of quiet, Megan jerked her

knot loose on Navigator's neck rope.

"Shh, what a good boy," she said.

One horse. Three girls. How would they escape the volcano?

Smoke billowed without ceasing from the crater above. But maybe it was just spouting off. This could be as bad as it was going to get.

"Navigator, you're the best," Darby told him.

With their hands and voices, all three girls soothed the big horse.

"Get on," Megan told Ann.

Suddenly, it was silent. The air around them was still and fragile as glass.

"I think it's stopped," Darby said, nodding toward the volcano.

"Can't trust it," Megan said, then she turned to Ann and her expression showed she was not up for an argument. "Go."

Ann flung herself at Navigator's back, hung there for a second, and then swung herself astride before reaching down for Darby's hand.

"He can carry all of us," Ann said, and she was probably right, but Darby couldn't climb on this way.

Hands shaking, Darby said, "I need a rock, or sidehill—"

"Quit fooling around!" Megan snapped. "Get on and meet me at camp!"

"Megan!" Darby yelled, but the older girl was already running, shouting something about the horses, over her shoulder.

A sound like the biggest tire in the world going flat hissed all around them.

"I thought that was a quiet volcano!" Darby yelled, and with a big jump, she made it onto the gelding's back.

"Moisture," Ann said. She didn't sound calm, but her hands were steady on the reins, letting Navigator pick the best path back down, letting him think everything was under control. "If they told us the truth, there'll be belches pretty soon. All the boys loved that," Ann said with a harsh laugh. "Yeah, these gassy explosions send hot rocks into the air"—Pele pelting her sister, Darby thought—"and then liquid rock, and then everything from inside that volcano just goes gushing every—"

The crack in the volcano's face reopened. This time a line of lava fountains appeared, sending a neon-orange spray up into the sky.

It was dark, and getting darker, Darby thought suddenly, and there was Megan, jogging and climbing parallel to them, taking a shorter route that was too cluttered with rocks for a horse.

A pop sounded. They looked back to see a single boulder arc into the sky, hang there like a planet, and then land in grass, leaving a comet's trail of fire in its wake.

"Hoku!" Darby yelled, and then she slammed her mouth closed.

Don't call her into danger, you idiot, she told herself.

"We have time," Ann said over her shoulder. She kept Navigator to a controlled pace, and Darby admired her levelheadedness. She knew galloping full out would panic the gelding further.

"Time?" Darby asked, squinting into the smoky gray world around her.

"There's no lava yet, and remember, when it comes, it's supposed to be slow, so we have time to get the horses and our packs."

Of course there was time to get the horses! What did Ann think, that she'd leave her filly tied up amid this nightmare?

"Yeah, but who cares about our packs?"

"Flashlights and food," Ann snapped. "We might be out here for a while."

Darby looked over her shoulder. Ann was right. She didn't see lava, but the two sisters wore halos of murky red. And there, jetting up from another crack, burned a bright and steady flame, consuming a small tree.

Darby was pretty sure they wouldn't need their flashlights. The world was lit with bright red light.

Chapter 18

Once Ann loosened the reins and let Navigator settle into his ground-eating lope, they reached camp in about three minutes.

"They're gone!" Darby gasped.

"They're here," Ann insisted. "It's just smoky and dark, hard—" Ann broke off, coughing. "Hard to see. There's Megan!"

Amazingly, the older girl emerged from the smoke, with a T-shirt tied over her face, leading Biscuit.

Darby slid off Navigator, even though she heard Ann's objection.

Lifting the hem of her own shirt to cover her nose and mouth, Darby blundered through the smoke.

There! She made out the rope line, but it lay on

the ground, torn free of a fallen ohia tree.

Why hadn't they tied the horses to the stone trees? Then Hoku and Sugarfoot wouldn't be gone.

Darby heard Ann shout her name a second before Navigator charged past, clipping her shoulder and knocking her down.

Navigator was even more upset than they were at the horses' disappearance. Plunging and wheeling, he searched and snorted. Darby jumped out of the way, seeing it was all Ann could do not to fall off.

Biscuit screamed nearby, and Darby felt Megan grab her forearm and haul her to her feet.

"—going after Hoku and—" Megan shouted, but rumbling covered half her words.

Darby nodded frantically. At least Hoku was safe. Gone, but out of the volcano's reach, with Megan on the way to help her.

Megan faced the buckskin, grabbed black mane, and vaulted aboard.

"—Navigator?" Megan yelled as the gelding lifted his front hooves, ready to flee.

"Yeah!" Darby called back, and then Megan and Biscuit were gone, and Navigator was right beside her.

"He wants to rear," Ann said levelly. "I think I can stop him, but give me a minute before you get on."

Darby squinted back uphill at the volcano's fiery glare.

"Get our packs," Ann said. "I'd do it, but I'm not

sure my leg can take the drop."

"Okay," Darby said, and she tried to concentrate on finding their packs, but she couldn't help staring at the top of Two Sisters. She tripped over a sleeping bag, fell to one knee, and looked uphill again.

The volcano had changed. There was a stream of orange, red, and yellow, mottled with black. And a smoke plume.

Or was it ash? Something moved down the slope, towering over her. Three stories high, it was shaped like gigantic gray broccoli and so huge, she lost her balance and had to look away. And then she laughed.

But there was something else within the broccoli form: a face with high cheekbones that looked furious.

Darby's laugh stopped as if someone had tied a gag over her mouth.

"Do you see that?" Darby asked, pointing.

"How could I not see it?" Ann demanded. "Don't get hysterical on me!"

"I won't." Darby snatched up Ann's backpack and looked around for hers.

"One is okay," Ann yelled over Navigator's loud snorting.

Somewhere, my mom is freaking out, Darby thought. She felt disconnected, as if she were floating above the campsite, watching. When had she felt that way before? She should know the answer to that question, but she couldn't remember.

Darby concentrated long enough to hand Ann's pack up to her.

Navigator misted her with his frantic breath and Darby felt guilty for bringing him into this nightmare.

Ann shrugged on the pack and gave the big bay a pat on the neck. "This is an amazing horse. Sugarfoot would've—"

Darby stopped listening and turned back. She broke into a jog as she spotted her own pack.

An explosion knocked her off her feet. The earth beneath her pitched. Was it an earthquake? Gas igniting? Magma churning up and overflowing the volcano's top?

Navigator reared, and it was a good thing he did.

A boulder the size of a beach ball whizzed through the night to land right where Darby had been standing, right where Navigator's front hooves had been, and fire flew behind it. Flames sprung up like golden dancers, following as the boulder rolled downhill.

The flames between Darby and Ann were only a foot high. Darby started to go around, but downhill, there was no path through, so she turned up the slope and ran, trying to reach the ground above the boulder's landing.

Clapping her heels to the frantic Navigator's ribs, Ann rode to meet her.

More quickly than the horse, fire fanned out

between them, wide as a car, and Navigator shied away, with sparks burning in his mane.

"Your hair!" Ann screamed.

For an instant, Darby could only see the firefly orange in Navigator's black mane, but then she heard sizzling. She clapped her hands to her own head. The spark only burned for an instant. And then she heard a neigh—not Navigator's—and the earth rumbled beneath her again, but not from the volcano.

A horse galloped through the smoke *on her side of the fire*, coming toward her.

Ann was screaming again, but Darby couldn't hear what she said.

Oh, no! Darby grabbed her stomach as if she'd been punched.

"Hoku!" The name burst from her before she could stop it.

Copper and cream, the filly ran toward her and then faltered as a wave of either smoke or ash swirled between them. She reared, trying to see over, and the tangerine-and-white lead rope dangled between her forelegs.

Why had Hoku come back to her? Safety lay downhill, away from this inferno.

"—tube!" Ann cried out.

At last Darby understood. They were divided by a widening wall of flame, but there were escape routes on each side. Ann and Navigator could make it to the road at the foot of the volcanic slope. With luck, that's what Megan had done.

Darby and Hoku, if they were very lucky, might make it through the lava tube, down to the beach near Sun House.

"Got it!" Darby shrieked, and she gulped back a laugh that became a cough.

Ann raised her hand, leaned low on Navigator's neck, and rode him down the slope.

Hoku circled Darby at a trot. The filly's eyes rolled white, staring at the fire, then focused on Darby as she tightened her bedraggled ponytail.

Hoku stopped. She nudged Darby's shoulder where the spark had burned through her hair. The mustang stared with confused intensity at her human.

"C'mon, girl." Darby tried to sound chipper, but she coughed again. Her asthma-scarred lungs fought the volcanic vapors. "Hoku, I'm just ripping off a piece of my T-shirt for a mask. *Shh*, girl," Darby soothed. "I'm no mouthless monster, just me. You know if I don't do it now, later might be too late."

Darby knotted the cloth over her nose and mouth. Her eyes never left her horse.

From ears to nostrils, the filly vibrated with fear. She looked down the slope, knowing that Navigator, Biscuit, and Sugarfoot were down there, though she couldn't possibly see the other horses. And then she walked to Darby.

Darby caught the lead rope, thankful beyond words that it was still there; that her horse was, for the moment, safe; and for the lava tube. She was pretty sure she could find it. There was a path, after all, and the fire cast plenty of light. She wouldn't get the flashlight from her pack until she needed it. Otherwise there was a chance she'd drop it, and she might not find her way through the lava tube in sheer darkness.

Lava. Squinting through the smoke, she saw it. A bright brass-colored snake of the burbling, hot liquid, edged in black, crawled toward them.

Mr. Silva had said that when lava cascaded down, the crater walls caved in and the lava flow slowed, then actually helped seal walls from outside with its overflow. She'd seen something like that once today. Maybe it was happening again.

Or maybe not. She couldn't assume that the brass-colored snake, which had broadened into a searing rope streaked with orange, would stop before it got to her. If it didn't, it would cut off her path to the lava tube, her last chance of escape.

Darby jogged as fast as she could. Even with her cloth mask, the air was like a hot, wet washcloth held against her face. She could barely breathe.

Hoku followed with total obedience, head bobbing as she trotted behind. Every now and then her hooves clipped the back of Darby's thick-soled boots, but she made no move to outpace the girl.

She wants to stay near me. She trusts me, but oh, she has no reason to—I have no idea what I'm doing, Darby thought.

"We've got to beat that river," Darby told her

horse, because that's what the orange-red lava stream had turned into. It spread thicker by the minute. Sparse grass and ohia trees ignited all around it, and it roared as it came.

Roaring. Lions' paws.

When Darby stopped to make the biggest decision of her life, Hoku moved alongside her, nudged her, and blew grainy breath down her neck.

Was Hoku telling her a secret, saying it was okay to ride her, to gallop from the lions' paws to the lava tube, outrunning Pele's fire?

Darby didn't turn to face her horse. She just reached up and touched the cheek alongside her own.

Can I do it?

In Nevada, she'd lain in the snow with the wild filly and talked her back from the brink of death. Instead of closing her dulled eyes and tumbling into darkness, Hoku had listened.

And tried.

And won.

Darby turned now and looked into her filly's golden face.

"Can you do it, girl? Can you carry me on your back?"

She led Hoku alongside the lions' paws. If the horse bolted while facing this direction, she'd be headed toward the mouth of the lava tube.

Holding the lead rope, Darby looked up to see lava smoking and crawling toward her. It was fire-edged now, an orange-red ribbon with flashes of gold and black. And hot. She and Hoku both dripped with sweat.

"It's time, baby girl," Darby said, and then she took a long step, climbing up onto the lava-rock lions' paws. Holding her breath, Darby eased her left leg slowly, inch by inch, over the filly's back.

Yes, the first time she got on her horse she did it backward, mounting from the right side. Just like the first time she'd mounted Navigator. If she told Jonah, she knew what he'd say. *Who told you it was wrong, the horse?*

Hoku's sleek, golden back hummed with energy. Darby felt the filly pondering this sudden change. It was familiar, but different. This time it didn't hurt. This time, it was comfort, not fear, which flowed into her from her rider.

Darby would have given her filly another minute to get used to carrying her, but Hoku's ribs flared beneath Darby's knees and a cough shook the horse. With a nervous glance at the lava, Hoku struck out, pawing with one forefoot.

"Let's get out of here, girl," Darby whispered, and leaned forward.

The filly took a tentative step, and then another and another. Each move was more sure, until she swung into a trot.

Please don't let me fall, Darby begged the stars overhead. *Please let me find the lava tunnel. Please let us get home safely.*

A cool breeze swept over them as they ran out of the lava's path and Hoku celebrated with a lope. Her hooves pelted grass and stone. Her legs swung strong and golden, forward and back, head level, belly almost skimming the ground, as if she knew exactly where she was going.

In the volcano's glare, Darby could barely make out Hoku's ears, hidden in the mane that rose and fell like creamy wave crests.

We can do this, Darby thought. Body balanced, hands wrapped in Hoku's mane, face pressed to her filly's neck, she felt like a centaur, half girl and half horse.

Just then, Darby heard tinkling beneath Hoku's hooves. The path was black among strands of silver. Tinkling, crackling, shattering. Pele's hair?

The filly slowed to a trot, then a walk. They were at the entrance to the lava tube, home free, if only she could get the flashlight from her backpack. Safe, if Hoku would go inside.

The filly neighed into the lava tube. The sound echoed. Hoku pawed at the hardened lava, trusting wild instincts that told her to keep going.

But why? It was unnatural for a wild horse to go into a dark, confined place. *Counterintuitive,* that was the word, Darby thought.

She felt dizzy and her mind spun. She was more at home in a world of words than here, trapped between a dangerous channel to the sea and blazing death.

Maybe wild horses had hidden here before and Hoku could smell them. Maybe Pele ran as a golden spirit within her filly. Maybe stars were the eyes of heaven, of ancestors who wanted Darby and Hoku to survive.

Darby fought for the advice of her logical mind. Should she ride in, or risk climbing off, get the flashlight from her backpack and walk? Get the flashlight and ride in?

The lava tube had a twelve-foot ceiling, isn't that what Megan had said?

Megan's face bobbed up in her mind. And then Ann's. And what if Jonah and the hands were out looking for her on the volcanic slope, amid all that fire and lava? No, Ann knew. She'd tell them Darby had gone through the lava tube. If Ann was okay.

Please let them be safe.

She left the flashlight in her backpack. If she dropped it, her horse could spook, whirl, and run the other way.

And she stayed on Hoku's back. Rather than risk falling from Hoku as she dismounted, she leaned forward and Hoku entered the lava tube as if she'd been there a million times before.

It was wet inside the tube—wetter than before. Darby could smell the moisture, and when Hoku stopped to lick the water from the stone walls, she touched them.

Shaking from the sudden change in temperature, she rode on.

Hoku's hoofbeats echoed all around her.

Something crawled across her brow! Was it a spider? Darby struck at it. A plant. A little tendril of root had made its way through the stone ceiling, looking for water.

The idea was only poignant for a second.

If a root could come through, so could liquid rock. Lava could drip down and burn them both.

Darby clucked, riding faster into the darkness.

What was that? Darby heard something behind them.

So did Hoku. The filly turned around of her own volition. She was either breathing hard or sucking in an unfamiliar scent.

It was probably just water dripping, Darby told herself.

"Back the other way, there's a beach," Darby murmured, trying to turn her horse with her knees. "You can run on the beach. You can swim. Keep going, girl."

Was lava oozing after her like a steady, red-hot boa constrictor?

She heard something else. Not lava. It sounded like a hammer shattering china dishes. And then a snort. Like Navigator?

At last, Darby knew she had to risk getting out her flashlight. Even if Hoku threw her here, they were safer than before.

She grappled for her pack. As she did, she realized there was a comfort in darkness. When she couldn't see, there were fewer things to fear.

But now, everything happened at once. Her fingers closed around her flashlight. She heard a snick of sound like a flashlight clicking on, but she hadn't done that yet. Darby lost her grip on her backpack. It hit the filly's legs on the way down and Hoku bolted as Darby flicked on the flashlight.

The beam surrounding her couldn't have been warm, but Darby imagined it was.

"Darby!" Ann's voice was a celebration, and then a gasp. "Oh my gosh, you're riding Hoku!"

All at once, the lava tube was crowded with white horses.

Ash, Darby thought. Ann's red hair was gray with it and she rode a pale Navigator with white Sugarfoot charging alongside.

Biscuit's black mane was powdered white as he pushed past the other horses to reach Hoku.

Biscuit was gliding his neck over Hoku's when Megan leaned over to shake Darby's shoulder. An ash cloud billowed off Darby's clothes and surrounded them, but it really didn't matter.

"Sister!" Megan said. Her voice spiraled high in joy, then broke into laughter as she took in Darby, mounted on Hoku. "The trouble some people will go to, to keep a secret!"

Chapter 19

"It's okay, girl!" Darby gasped.

With the greetings over, Hoku suddenly felt cramped. She lashed out a hind hoof and it struck the lava tube's wall.

"You're doing so well. No one means to scare you."

"Boy, this is a day to remember," Ann said.

Darby nodded.

The first day she'd ridden Hoku. . . .

Darby knew she would never have forgotten it anyway, but she wished the volcano hadn't made it quite so memorable.

Hoku rocked backward in a half-rear and Darby ducked, holding tight to her horse's neck.

"I think I'll get off and lead her," Darby said as Hoku came back down to all four hooves.

"I think that would get you trampled," Megan said.

In the crazy flashlight shadows, Darby realized the hammer she'd heard destroying china plates had actually been those twelve hooves clattering on the lava stone.

"It's not that far to the beach," Ann said. "Listen."

Darby held her breath until she heard the same sound she'd listened to by holding a seashell to her ear. The beach was out there, and Jonah had said Sun House could be sighted from that beach.

"The mask's a good idea," Megan interrupted. "Don't take it off. When two-thousand-degree lava hits the ocean, it dissolves the salt and makes hydrochloric acid."

"Not good for someone with asthma," Ann tried to joke.

"Not good for anyone," Megan said, and the next time she spoke, they were all masked with ripped pieces of clothing.

It was a relief, and Megan's voice cut into the waves' purling, "Will you tell Jonah?"

"I hadn't thought about it yet," Darby said. "I was just thinking we'd better check the horses over as soon as we get out of here. I mean, sparks sizzled my hair and burned a hole in my shirt. . . ."

Darby stopped chattering, seeing Jonah's face in smoke just as she'd seen Pele's.

"Well, you better think about it," Megan said. "I don't mean to sound mean," she added as Ann whipped around to look at her. "It's just, I'm sure they're all out looking for us, and it just makes sense that he'd be the one to come down here."

"I don't think I should tell him yet, or let him see me riding Hoku, until she's perfect," Darby said.

"So, you think you'll still be riding when you're ninety?" Ann teased. "Darby, no horse is perfect. Neither are riders."

"I know, but he doesn't think much of mustangs, and she's not that good around men. . . ."

"You can count on me to keep your secret, if that's what you want to do," Megan said, "but don't forget he already thought, last week, that she was ready to carry a rider."

"Yeah," Darby said, but Megan hadn't been there when Jonah had barked *I wash my hands of you*, just because she'd fallen off Navigator.

His words had sliced through her like knives.

If Hoku acted up in front of him . . .

Ann clucked and the horses moved forward in the lava tube.

Darby tried not to think about what would happen if Hoku threw her as Jonah watched. They'd have to prove themselves all over again, and though her filly had the spirit for another test, Darby wasn't sure she did.

❋ ❋ ❋

It somehow felt like forever, but also felt like she'd just ducked into the lava tube when the three girls and four horses emerged from the darkness into a moonlit night of waves, stars, and steam hissing and rising into the air.

Lava flowed into the ocean no more than a quarter mile up the coast from them, and Darby could hear the sea boiling.

"The wind's with us," Megan said, pointing at a huge steam cloud blowing over the sea, not ashore.

But the horses were staring at the ocean right in front of them. They showed no inclination to gallop into the water.

"That fizzing and hissing doesn't belong in the ocean, and they know it," Ann said as she slid off Navigator's bare back.

Darby gave a short laugh as she remembered Jonah saying that he and Kit had determined that Darby shouldn't waste Hoku's curiosity. The filly had learned a year's worth of information about wild Hawaii today.

Darby's knees buckled as she slid off her horse, and she ended up holding the rope, sitting in the sand, looking up at Hoku.

Moonlight painted the star on the filly's chest, making it brighter than usual. Beyond Hoku, a black shoulder of land showed. Bright lava went gliding into the sea as if Pele had let it flow from her open hand, across her palm, over her fingertips, into the water.

Pele wasn't a woman in a red convertible, Darby thought. Pele was nature, both fierce and gentle. *We escaped because we didn't intrude. If we'd been gazing into the crater, it wouldn't have been like looking into the flames of a campfire. When the eruption came, we would have gone up in flames.*

A sea bird sailed overhead, crying a night song. Despite her morbid thoughts, Darby wanted time to stop. She could stay on the black velvet beach forever, unless the wind shifted.

Holding each other's mounts, the girls took off their masks, then rushed through the job of checking the horses for injuries. All of the horses' manes and the girls' hair had crispy places where sparks had burned them, and Sugarfoot had a skinned knee.

"He did that when he made his split-second decision to come back," Ann guessed.

Ann's remark set off a question in Darby's mind, but she didn't circle back to it until they'd remounted, ponying Hoku, and they were on their way down the beach, toward the barely visible lights of Sun House.

"Why did you guys come back uphill? Did you get cut off by fire before you reached the road?" Darby forked her fingers through Navigator's mane. "Was the road covered with lava or something?" She was straightening the gelding's reins, trying not to think about the bumps of his backbone, when she noticed the silence.

Megan and Ann gave her such accusing stares,

they were plain to read by moonlight.

"What?" Darby asked.

"It didn't look all bad down below," Ann said.

"Well then, why—" Darby's frustration rose, but Megan cut her off.

"We came back for you!"

"Why?" Darby demanded. "What were you thinking? You had a safe—okay, relatively safe—way out of that"—she searched for an appropriate word—"I don't know, firestorm, that was behind you. Why would you walk right back into danger when I was okay?"

"We weren't sure you were okay—" Megan started.

"I don't like my friends to put themselves in mortal danger," Darby interrupted.

"We weren't in mortal danger," Ann said in a humoring tone.

"Of course we were," Megan said, then she rode Biscuit into Navigator's path and held Darby quiet with a stare. "The last time Ann saw you, you were on foot and we didn't know what would happen with Hoku. You love her. You might have taken some risks to protect her."

"I mean, she's wild. What were the odds you were going to jump on and ride her bareback, with lava at your heels?" Ann asked.

Hoku whinnied and the girls laughed. Then the mustang tossed her flaxen mane and gave an even longer neigh.

"She's a smart girl," Darby said, smooching at the sorrel filly.

Seeing another horse getting attention, Sugarfoot pranced, bidding for Ann's praise.

"Of course, it was all Sugarfoot's idea. He saw you follow that white stallion into the lava tube and he had to go chase him."

"What?" Darby asked. "We didn't follow the white stallion. I haven't seen him since he jumped over us up there." Darby gestured in the direction of the stone pulpit where they'd hidden to watch Black Lava and his herd.

Ann was shrugging, as if she didn't want to start another spat, when a voice boomed out of the darkness and a mounted silhouette cut its way down a sand dune.

"You girls done playing with fire? Decided to come back on home and let the old folks quit worrying?"

"Jonah!" Darby shouted. She tapped Navigator with her heels and the other girls rode beside her until they drew rein in front of Kona.

"You girls all right?" her grandfather asked. "Horses come through that okay?"

"We're fine," Megan said. "We managed to sidestep the whole thing."

Ann made a half-strangled sound of disbelief.

"Well, okay, maybe not the whole thing," Megan amended. "But none of us have anything worse than crispy hair—"

"From the sparks," Ann explained. "Except Sugarfoot's knee, but I'll just clean that up and put a little salve on it."

Jonah seemed to notice that Darby hadn't said anything since she'd shouted his name.

"How you doing, Granddaughter? Trip to Two Sisters all you hoped for?"

Megan and Ann were laughing when Darby blurted, "I rode Hoku."

She hadn't meant to say it.

It was quiet for a long time, except that hooves hit sand and waves searched the shore. Darby imagined Jonah's face changing colors as he tried to keep his temper under control.

"How'd she do?" Jonah asked at last.

"Perfect. It's like she understood I had no choice."

Darby winced at her own words. That had definitely been the wrong thing to say. It sounded like she hadn't been in control.

"I always knew that Three Bars breeding would shine through when it counted," her grandfather said.

But this time Darby was too proud of her horse to let Jonah's comment go.

"Not to mention her mustang instincts," Darby said.

"Could be," Jonah shrugged, and Hoku chose that moment to snake her head out and snap toward Jonah's stirrup. "Remind that broomtail of yours who pays for the hay she loves."

"Hoku," Darby said in a scolding tone, but then Jonah changed his mind.

"Never mind. Actions speak louder than words. Animals get that sooner than people. She'll come around to tolerating me, after a while."

Hooves splatted on the wet beach. They rode for another minute before Jonah glanced at the glowing display of his cell phone.

"Oh, I bet my parents are out looking for me!" Ann said suddenly.

"Them and Kit, Cade, and Kimo. Cathy's holding up her end by going crazy and sayin' she told me so," Jonah said.

"But I bet she's on the lanai with binoculars," Megan said. She made a huge waving motion and yelled, "Hi, Mom!"

When Sugarfoot and Hoku shied, Megan said, "Sorry!"

"Try to call them again, please," Ann urged Jonah.

"The news is saying this is a minor eruption, just the hot sister lettin' off steam," Jonah said.

Darby felt relieved. Even though it had felt like a hellish inferno to her, maybe her mother wouldn't be too worried.

She was swaying comfortably on Navigator's bare back, feeling proud of her horse and herself, when she caught Jonah watching her.

Embarrassed and hopelessly empty of things to say, Darby opened her mouth, but nothing came out.

"That's got it," Jonah said, but he'd stopped looking at Darby. He was pressing a button on his cell phone.

First he called Aunty Cathy to let her know they were riding home. Next, he called Ed and Ramona Potter. Then he made a third call.

"Hey, Kit," Jonah shouted as if he could communicate to the other side of the island by volume alone. "Yeah. All of 'em. Called you first, but you can tell Kimo and Cade"—Jonah glanced over at Darby and gave her a wink—"the can-do *keiki* is back in the barn."

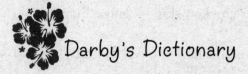
Darby's Dictionary

In case anybody reads this besides me, which it's too late to tell you not to do if you've gotten this far, I know this isn't a real dictionary. For one thing, it's not all correct, because I'm just adding things as I hear them. Besides, this dictionary is just to help me remember. Even though I'm pretty self-conscious about pronouncing Hawaiian words, it seems to me if I live here (and since I'm part Hawaiian), I should at least try to say things right.

ali'i — AH LEE EE — royalty, but it includes chiefs besides queens and kings and people like that 'aumakua — OW MA KOO AH — these are family guardians from ancient times. I think ancestors are supposed to come back and look out for their family members. Our 'aumakua are owls and Megan's is a sea turtle.

chicken skin — goose bumps

da kine — DAH KYNE — "that sort of thing" or "stuff like that"

hanai — HA NYE E — a foster or adopted child, like Cade is Jonah's, but I don't know if it's permanent

haole — HOWLEE — a foreigner, especially a white person. I get called that, or *hapa* (half) *haole*, even though I'm part Hawaiian.

hewa-hewa — HEE VAH HEE VAH — crazy

hiapo — HIGH AH PO — a firstborn child, like me, and it's apparently tradition for grandparents, if they feel like it, to just take hiapo to raise!

hoku — HO COO — star

holoholo — HOE LOW HOW LOW — a pleasure trip that could be a walk, a ride, a sail, etc.

honu — HO NEW — sea turtle

'iolani — EE OH LAWN EE — this is a hawk that brings messages from the gods, but Jonah has it painted on his trucks as an owl bursting through the clouds

ipo — EE POE — sweetheart, actually short for *ku'uipo*

kapu — KAH POO — forbidden, a taboo

lanai — LAH NA E — this is like a balcony or veranda. Sun House's is more like a long balcony with a view of the pastures.

lau hala — LA OO HA LA — some kind of leaf in shades of brown, used to make paniolo hats like Cade's. I guess they're really expensive.

lei — LAY E — necklace of flowers. I thought they were pronounced LAY, but Hawaiians add another sound. I also thought leis were sappy touristy things, but getting one is a real honor, from the right people.

lei niho palaoa — LAY NEEHO PAH LAHOAH — necklace made for old-time Hawaiian royalty from braids of their own hair. It's totally *kapu*—forbidden—for anyone else to wear it.

<u>luna</u> — LOU NUH — a boss or top guy, like Jonah's stallion

<u>menehune</u> — MEN AY WHO NAY — little people

<u>ohia</u> — OH HE UH — a tree like the one next to Hoku's corral

<u>pali</u> — PAW LEE — cliffs

<u>paniolo</u> — PAW KNEE OH LOW — cowboy or cowgirl

<u>pau</u> — POW — finished, like Kimo is always asking, "You *pau*?" to see if I'm done working with Hoku or shoveling up after the horses

<u>Pele</u> — PAY LAY — the volcano goddess. Red is her color. She's destructive with fire, but creative because she molds lava into new land. She's easily offended if you mess with things sacred to her, like the ohia tree, lehua flowers, 'ohelo berries, and the wild horse herd on Two Sisters.

<u>pueo</u> — POO AY OH — an owl, our family guardian. The very coolest thing is that one lives in

the tree next to Hoku's corral.

<u>pupule</u> — POO POO LAY — crazy

<u>tutu</u> — TOO TOO — great-grandmother

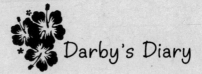
Darby's Diary

Ellen Kealoha Carter—my mom, and since she's responsible for me being in Hawaii, I'm putting her first. Also, I miss her. My mom is a beautiful and talented actress, but she hasn't had her big break yet. Her job in Tahiti might be it, which is sort of ironic because she's playing a Hawaiian for the first time and she swore she'd never return to Hawaii. And here I am. I get the feeling she had huge fights with her dad, Jonah, but she doesn't hate Hawaii.

Cade—fifteen or so, he's Jonah's adopted son. Jonah's been teaching him all about being a paniolo. I thought he was Hawaiian, but when he took off his hat he had blond hair—in a braid! Like old-time vaqueros—weird! He doesn't go to school, just takes his classes by correspondence through the mail. He wears this poncho that's almost black it's such a dark green, and he blends in with the forest. Kind of creepy the way he just appears out there. Not counting Kit, Cade might be the best rider on the ranch.

Hoku kicked him in the chest. I wish she hadn't. He told me that his stepfather beat him all the time.

<u>Cathy Kato</u>—forty or so? She's the ranch manager and, really, the only one who seems to manage Jonah. She's Megan's mom and the widow of a paniolo, Ben. She has messy blond-brown hair to her chin, and she's a good cook, but she doesn't think so. It's like she's just pulling herself back together after Ben's death.

I get the feeling she used to do something with advertising or public relations on the mainland.

<u>Jonah Kaniela Kealoha</u>—my grandfather could fill this whole notebook. Basically, though, he's harsh/nice, serious/funny, full of legends and stories about magic, but real down-to-earth. He's amazing with horses, which is why they call him the Horse Charmer. He's not that tall, maybe 5'8", with black hair that's getting gray, and one of his fingers is still kinked where it was broken by a teacher because he spoke Hawaiian in class! I don't like his "don't touch the horses unless they're working for you" theory, but it totally works. I need to figure out why.

<u>Kimo</u>—he's so nice! I guess he's about twenty-five, Hawaiian, and he's just this sturdy, square, friendly guy. He drives in every morning from his house over by Crimson Vale, and even though he's late a lot, I've never seen anyone work so hard.

<u>Kit Ely</u>—the ranch foreman, the boss, next to Jonah. He's Sam's friend Jake's brother and a real buckaroo. He's about 5'10" with black hair. He's half Shoshone, but he could be mistaken for Hawaiian, if he wasn't always promising to whip up a batch of Nevada chili and stuff like that. And he wears a totally un-Hawaiian leather string with brown-streaked turquoise stones around his neck. He got to be foreman through his rodeo friend Pani (Ben's buddy). Kit's left wrist got pulverized in a rodeo fall. He's still amazing with horses, though.

<u>Megan Kato</u>—Cathy's fifteen-year-old daughter, a super athlete with long reddish-black hair. She's beautiful and popular and I doubt she'd be my friend if we just met at school. Maybe, though, because she's nice at heart. She half makes fun of Hawaiian legends, then turns around and acts really serious about them. Her Hawaiian name is Mekana.

<u>The Zinks</u>—they live on the land next to Jonah. They have barbed-wire fences and their name doesn't sound Hawaiian, but that's all I know.

<u>Tutu</u>—my great-grandmother. She lives out in the rain forest like a medicine woman or something, and she looks like my mom will when she's old. She has a pet owl.

<u>Aunt Babe Borden</u>—Jonah's sister, so she's really my great-aunt. She owns half of the family land, which is divided by a border that runs between the Two Sisters. Aunt Babe and Jonah don't get along, and though she's fashionable and caters to rich people at her resort, she and her brother are identically stubborn. Aunt Babe pretends to be all business, but she loves her cremello horses and I think she likes having me and Hoku around.

<u>Duxelles Borden</u>—if you lined up all the people on Hawaii and asked me to pick out one NOT related to me, it would be Duxelles, but it turns out she's my cousin. Tall (I come up to her shoulders), strong, and with this metallic blond hair, she's popular despite being a bully. She lives with Aunt Babe while her mom travels with her dad, who's a world-class kayaker. About the only thing Duxelles and I have in common is we're both swimmers. Oh, and I gave her a nickname—Duckie.

❦ ANIMALS! ❧

<u>Hoku</u>—my wonderful sorrel filly! She's about two and a half years old, a full sister to the Phantom, and boy, does she show it! She's fierce (hates men) but smart, and a one-girl (ME!) horse for sure. She is definitely a herd-girl, and when it comes to choosing between me and other horses, it's a real toss-up. Not that I blame her. She's run free for a long time, and I don't want to take away what makes her special.

She loves hay, but she's really HEAD-SHY due to Shan Stonerow's early "training," which, according to Sam, was beating her.

Hoku means "star." Her dam is Princess Kitty, but her sire is a mustang named Smoke and he's mustang all the way back to a "white renegade with murder in his eye" (Mrs. Allen).

<u>Navigator</u>—my riding horse is a big, heavy Quarter Horse that reminds me of a knight's charger. He has Three Bars breeding (that's a big deal), but when he picked me, Jonah let him keep me! He's black with rusty rings around his eyes and a rusty muzzle. (Even though he looks black, the proper description is brown, they tell me.) He can find his way home from any place on the island. He's sweet, but no pushover. Just when I think he's sort of a safety net for my beginning riding skills, he tests me.

Joker—Cade's Appaloosa gelding is gray splattered with black spots and has a black mane and tail. He climbs like a mountain goat and always looks like he's having a good time. I think he and Cade have a history, maybe Jonah took them in together?

Biscuit—buckskin gelding, one of Ben's horses, a dependable cow pony. Kit rides him a lot.

Hula Girl—chestnut cutter

Blue Ginger—blue roan mare with tan foal

Honolulu Lulu—bay mare

Tail Afire (Koko)—fudge brown mare with silver mane and tail

Blue Moon—Blue Ginger's baby

Moonfire—Tail Afire's baby

Black Cat—Lady Wong's black foal

Luna Dancer—Hula Girl's bay baby

Honolulu Half Moon

Conch—grulla cow pony, gelding, needs work. Megan rides him sometimes.

Kona—big gray, Jonah's cow horse

Luna—beautiful, full-maned bay stallion is king of 'Iolani Ranch. He and Jonah seem to have a bond.

Lady Wong—dappled gray mare and Kona's dam. Her current foal is Black Cat.

Australian shepherds—pack of five: Bart, Jack, Jill, Peach, and Sass

Pipsqueak/Pip—little shaggy white dog that runs with the big dogs, belongs to Megan and Cathy

Tango—Megan's once-wild rose roan mare. I think she and Hoku are going to be pals.

Sugarfoot—Ann Potter's horse is a beautiful Morab (half Morgan and half Arabian, she told me). He's a caramel-and-white paint with one white foot. He can't be used with "clients" at the Potters' because he's a chaser. Though Ann and her mother, Ramona, have pretty much schooled it out of him, he's still not quite trustworthy. If he ever chases me, I'm supposed to stand my ground, whoop, and holler. Hope I never have to do it!

Flight—this cremello mare belongs to Aunt Babe (she has a whole herd of cremellos) and nearly died of longing for her foal. She was a totally different horse—beautiful and spirited—once she got him back!

Stormbird—Flight's cream-colored (with a blush of palomino) foal with turquoise eyes has had an exciting life for a four-month-old. He's been shipwrecked, washed ashore, fended for himself, and rescued.

✿ PLACES ✿

Lehua High School—the school Megan and I go to. School colors are red and gold.

Crimson Vale—it's an amazing and magical place, and once I learn my way around, I bet I'll love it. It's like a maze, though. Here's what I know: From town you can go through the valley or take the ridge road—valley has lily pads, waterfalls, wild horses, and rainbows. The ridge route (Pali?) has sweeping turns that almost made me sick. There are black rock teeter-totter-looking things that are really ancient altars and a SUDDEN drop-off down to a white sand beach. Hawaiian royalty are supposedly buried in the cliffs.

<u>Moku Lio Hihiu</u> — Wild Horse Island, of course!

<u>Mountain to the Sky</u> — sometimes just called Sky Mountain. Goes up to 5,000 feet, sometimes gets snow, and Megan said there used to be wild horses there.

<u>The Two Sisters</u> — cone-shaped "mountains." A border-line between them divides Jonah's land from his sister's — my great-aunt Babe. One of them is an active volcano. Kind of scary.

<u>Sun House</u> — our family place. They call it plantation style, but it's like a sugar plantation, not a Southern mansion. It has an incredible lanai that overlooks pastures all the way to Mountain to the Sky and Two Sisters. Upstairs is this little apartment Jonah built for my mom, but she's never lived in it.

<u>Hapuna</u> — biggest town on island, has airport, flag-pole, public and private schools, etc., palm trees, and coconut trees

'Iolani Ranch—our home ranch. 2,000 acres, the most beautiful place in the world.

Pigtail Fault—Near the active volcano. It looks more like a steam vent to me, but I'm no expert. According to Cade, it got its name because a poor wild pig ended up head down in it and all you could see was his tail. Too sad!

Sugar Sands Cove Resort—Aunt Babe and her polo-player husband, Phillipe, own this resort on the island. It has sparkling white buildings and beaches and a four-star hotel. The most important thing to me is that Sugar Sands Cove Resort has the perfect water-schooling beach for me and Hoku.

❧ ON THE RANCH, THERE ARE ❧
PASTURES WITH NAMES LIKE:

Sugar Mill and Upper Sugar Mill—for cattle

Two Sisters—for young horses, one- and two-year-olds they pretty much leave alone

Flatland—mares and foals

Pearl Pasture—borders the rain forest, mostly two- and three-year-olds in training

<u>Borderlands</u> — saddle herd and Luna's compound

I guess I should also add me . . .

<u>Darby Leilani Kealoha Carter</u> — I love horses more than anything, but books come in second. I'm thirteen, and one-quarter Hawaiian, with blue eyes and black hair down to about the middle of my back. On a good day, my hair is my best feature. I'm still kind of skinny, but I don't look as sickly as I did before I moved here. I think Hawaii's curing my asthma. Fingers crossed.

I have no idea what I did to land on Wild Horse Island, but I want to stay here forever.

Darby and Hoku's adventures continue in . . .

SEA SHADOW

Sea Shadow

$\mathcal{H}$ow did horses put up with riding in dizzying Tilt-A-Whirl horse trailers?

Darby Carter clung to the partition between herself and Hoku as the truck and trailer made a sickening swoop around a pond-sized puddle.

At first, it had seemed like a good idea to ride in the trailer with Hoku, so she could see firsthand how it felt. And from inside the truck, she couldn't read her filly's eyes or ears. So Darby had chosen this short drive from 'Iolani Ranch to Sugar Sands Cove Resort to give it a try.

Gazing through the open-sided trailer into the tropical forest, Darby decided a better question than how horses put up with such treatment was *why*?

They were bigger and stronger than the humans who asked them to go inside these wheeled torture chambers.

Hoku's neck wrinkled like sorrel satin as she turned to regard Darby. Blinking and chewing her hay, the filly looked puzzled by her human's staggering.

"I only have two legs to balance on," Darby explained to her mustang. "You can brace with all four."

Hoku swallowed. She kept her eyes on Darby's and her ears pricked forward for more conversation.

"Besides, horses must have a different sort of inner ear than humans. Otherwise, a rowdy girl like you would never get in a horse trailer for a second trip."

Hoku broke off their stare by nudging Darby's nose with her own.

Darby stumbled back, hit the far side of the trailer, and slid down to the floor. She rubbed her nose and considered the trailer from this new angle. It was a good thing she'd scrubbed every inch of it clean before deciding to ride back here.

The truck and trailer made another swoop and this time the maneuver not only left her stomach someplace back down the road, it sprayed her with muddy water. Darby wiped her cheeks and tried to visualize Sugar Sands Cove.

The trip would be worth it. After a week of rain

that had turned 'Iolani Ranch into a swamp, the warm white beach would be heavenly.

She was still amazed that her grandfather, Jonah, had allowed her to get up early and do this on a school day. Once they arrived, there wouldn't be time to do much except unload Hoku and head for the waves.

Darby sighed. She never would have been able to go swimming with a horse before school when she lived in Pacific Pinnacles, California. Only on Wild Horse Island did things like this happen!

She was imagining the sandy warmth against her bare feet and Hoku's hooves, when dirt scratched the tires, pebbles pinged under the trailer, and the truck came to a halt that slammed her teeth together.

Enough.

"Cade!" Darby shrieked.

She'd been so eager to continue Hoku's sea schooling, she'd agreed to let the teenage cowboy drive.

"What are you doing?" she demanded when he didn't answer.

Jonah thought it was no big deal for Cade, who hadn't tested for his driver's license yet, to make short trips like this. Her grandfather often needed more help around the ranch than he had, so Cade did things like this all the time. Driving for agricultural purposes was even legal if he kept to the unpaved private roads belonging to 'Iolani Ranch.

Legal was one thing. Safe was another.

The truck door squeaked open. Why was Cade getting out of the truck?

Darby had opened her mouth to ask, when Cade's shadow blocked the sunlight streaming into the trailer.

"Stay down and stay quiet."

Hoku must have been as surprised as Darby, because the filly didn't flatten her ears or kick the tailgate.

Darby rarely obeyed orders without asking why, but this time she made an exception. Cade's grim whisper kept her seated and silent.

As Cade's boots moved away, Darby pictured the lanky guy with his blond paniolo braid tucked under his hat. She heard him striding around mud puddles, moving determinedly toward—what? An injured animal he didn't want her to see? A place where the road had washed out?

Darby calculated that they'd driven about halfway to Aunt Babe's resort. That meant they were passing near the taro fields.

Hoku's uneasy nicker muffled the sound of a second pair of feet.

"Good way to get run over, blocking the road like that," Cade said.

Who was he talking to?

Getting to her feet to peek out of the trailer was almost irresistible, but Darby managed to stay down.

"What's in the trailer?"

The oily voice made Darby glad she hadn't moved. Cade's stepfather Manny was out there. He owned the taro fields, so it made sense that he'd be in the area.

Logic didn't stop Darby's goose bumps.

Kimo had said Manny reminded him of a pit bull and Megan had said Manny's head looked like a coconut—round with dark, stringy hair.

Darby's mind didn't pull up a clear picture of Manny; just the information that he hurt horses and children, and the feeling that he was the scariest man she'd ever met.

Why had he decided to block the road? And why should he care what was in the trailer?

"Horse I'm taking over to the tourist trap," Cade said, and Darby could tell he thought that if he could get Manny to poke fun at Babe's fancy resort, he'd stay away from the trailer.

It didn't work.

"Which horse?" Manny's voice moved closer. His shadow blocked the light.

Hoku drew back in surprise, but just for a second. Nostrils flaring, she lunged, colliding with the metal wall of the trailer.

"That filly from Nevada."

This time Cade's casual tone sounded strained. Was he afraid Manny had seen her? Had he?

So what? Darby asked herself. Manny was a

small, mean man who stole ancient Hawaiian arti-
facts and sold them on the black market. Not a kid-
napper.

"The one with the white . . ."

Darby didn't catch the rest of what Manny said,
but her gaze lifted to the white star on Hoku's chest,
the marking she'd named her for, and she wished
Manny hadn't known that detail about her horse.

"How'd Mom do in the earthquakes?" Cade
asked.

He might be trying to distract his stepfather, but
Darby heard the real concern in Cade's voice. Not
that Dee deserved it.

Be fair, Darby told herself, but she couldn't.

She'd never met the woman who'd allowed
Manny to beat Cade until his jaw was broken, but
that was all Darby needed to know to dislike Cade's
mom.

"Dee's fine," Manny spat, "but the house is a
wreck. Roof came down on the lanai. Stuff broke.
You'd think she was homeless the way she carries
on."

"All you need to do is call the state. They'll come
out and tag—"

"Yeah, I want the state digging into my business,"
Manny sneered. There was a moment of quiet interrupted by the agitated call of a bird, before Manny
went on. "You know, your mom coulda been out of
here, livin' in luxury on the mainland. It's your fault

she's not. All you had to do was turn over that colt."

That colt?

Stormbird! Darby thought, and all at once she remembered the midnight phone call she'd eavesdropped on from her bedroom. Jonah had called Cade in from the bunkhouse, telling him it was his mother. It probably had been, at first, but Darby remembered the surly tone in Cade's voice when she'd been sure he'd been talking to Manny.

"I'm never putting any horse in your hands ever again."

"Like you have a choice."

If a venomous snake had a hissing voice, this would be it.

"You don't scare me," Cade insisted.

"Don't have to. I have title to that Appy of yours."

Darby knew that a title was a legal paper saying you owned something, like a boat or a car or a horse. She and her mother had gotten Hoku through the Bureau of Land Management's wild horse adoption program, and even though they'd been permitted to take the filly out of state, they wouldn't have legal title to her until after next Christmas.

Manny owned Joker. That was awful, but what did it have to do with Stormbird?

Darby could almost hear the thudding of Cade's heart as he thought about his horse. He loved Joker. She'd heard him call the Appaloosa "brother."

"Well, he's back with Babe now," Cade said.

He . . . they had to be talking about Stormbird again.

"Babe hasn't given you and your little girlfriends the reward yet." Manny's wheedling tone made Darby grit her teeth. "That reward will buy you the title to Joker. He'll be yours, free and clear."

"I'll think about it," Cade said.

"Don't think small."

"What's that supposed to mean?"

"It'll take the whole reward to get your horse."

"But, it's a three-way split," Cade sounded confused.

"Stuff happens," Manny said.

Cade made a disgusted sound. "I'm *hanai*'d to Jonah. You agreed to that. And one of the girls is his granddaughter —"

"Saw her. Don't trust her."

He doesn't trust me? Darby pressed her hands over her mouth to smother her squeak of outrage.

"She'd be heartbroken to hear she don't have your admiration," Cade snapped, but that didn't stop Manny.

"Now, Mekana? Give her problems and she'd kick your butt. But that Darby girl's like a monkey, yeah? More going on in her head than she lets on — What was that?"

Darby didn't think she'd uttered a peep, but why else would Manny sound so suspicious?

"Never heard a filly squeal before?" Cade was

making fun of his stepfather, but Manny's feet still moved closer.

As he approached, Hoku uttered a high-pitched whinny. The whites of her eyes showed as she struck out a hoof in warning.

Good girl. Darby sent her thoughts flowing toward the mustang. *Smart girl.*

"Yeah, well," Manny seemed to lose interest. "You know where to find me. . . .".

"So I stay away," Cade told him.

". . . And I know where to find that Appy."

Darby thought she heard Manny leave on some small vehicle like an all-terrain vehicle, but she wasn't going to make a move until Cade told her it was just the three of them again.

She'd been so still for so long, sitting with her arms wrapped around her knees, her joints felt stiff. But it gave Darby time to wonder what she'd do if she were Cade.

It was easy to forget he had been an abused child. Jonah had told her about seeing ten-year-old Cade running away from home. He'd been walking along the road, his broken jaw swollen to the size of a grapefruit, leading Joker with a belt around his neck. Not everyone who'd had that kind of treatment would turn out honest and hardworking like Cade.

But this was a tough decision. Making a decision between honesty and your horse was kind of a cross-road, and putting herself in Cade's position wasn't hard. She'd gladly give up her part of the reward, and try to persuade Megan and Cade to do the same, if it meant keeping Hoku out of the hands of a creep like Manny.

Discover all the adventures on
Wild Horse Island!

THE HORSE CHARMER
TERRI FARLEY

THE SHINING STALLION
TERRI FARLEY

RAIN FOREST ROSE
TERRI FARLEY

CASTAWAY COLT
TERRI FARLEY

FIRE MAIDEN
TERRI FARLEY

HarperTrophy®
An Imprint of HarperCollinsPublishers

www.harpercollinschildrens.com